WREATH FOR A REDHEAD

If redhead Cheryl Vickers thought she could blackmail a prominent industrialist like Benedict Van Huizen, she was mistaken. Mark Preston was called in, and he soon found himself dealing with double murder. As usual, the dames complicated everything. Van Huizen's lovely wife, Marcia, was fooling around with an ex-fighter. Gorgeous Rona Parsons came in from San Francisco to make sure Preston stayed interested in the case. Denver Morley came in too, but he was holding a gun — in Preston's direction.

PETER CHAMBERS

WREATH FOR A REDHEAD

Complete and Unabridged

LINFORD
Leicester

First published in Great Britain in 1962

First Linford Edition
published 2003

British Library CIP Data

Chambers, Peter, *1924* –
    Wreath for a redhead.—Large print ed.—
Linford mystery library
    1. Detective and mystery stories
    2. Large type books
    I. Title
    823.9′14 [F]

    ISBN 1–8439–5012–X

Published by
F. A. Thorpe (Publishing)
Anstey, Leicestershire

Set by Words & Graphics Ltd.
Anstey, Leicestershire
Printed and bound in Great Britain by
T. J. International Ltd., Padstow, Cornwall

This book is printed on acid-free paper

1

I only ever saw Cheryl Vickers once, but she wasn't a girl a man would forget in a hurry. The meeting was arranged one stifling Tuesday morning in July. Every window in the office was open, in contravention of the tenancy regulations, which claimed to keep the place cool by air-conditioning.

My light-weight jacket was thrown across a chair and the collar button of my shirt was open. Any air there was around must be reserved for very privileged people, and it didn't seem that I figured on the list. I stood by the corner window, the one where you get a view of the Pacific Ocean. The water looked a cool blue. Anybody with any sense in his head would be down at the beach end of town, all dressed up in a pocket handkerchief and idling around in the surf. The pavements gleamed white, and I noticed a couple of guys doing a repaint job on a store front. The colour chosen was a pale yellow, and although the painters were wearing dark glasses, I didn't feel any desire to trade places with them. In any case, I had to stay right where I was. There was a visitor on the way. His name was Dean Hillier, and he'd telephoned about an hour before to say he'd be in at eleven. It was almost that now. I tried another glass of iced water, but it just didn't hit the spot. The buzzer sounded, and when I didn't move fast enough, it buzzed again, longer. I didn't blame Florence Digby if she was a little short in the temper today. Her office must have been ten degrees hotter than mine. I flicked down the key.

'Keep cool, Miss Digby.'

Her voice had the carefully measured tone of someone who was holding on to her patience.

'Mr. Hillier is here, Mr. Preston.'

'O.K. Float him in.'

He was twenty-eight or so, a well-distributed hundred and eighty, about five eleven. The black hair was crewcut, and the regular features were clean shaven. He was dressed in a light-grey linen suit, expensive, white shirt ditto, green woollen tie. The black leather shoes were a trifle heavy for the weather, but anybody could see Mr. Hillier was the well-dressed business guy, and a prosperous business, too.

'Glad to know you, Mr. Hillier.'

He shook hands firmly enough and took the chair I indicated.

'Kind of hot,' I offered.

'It certainly is.' His voice was like the rest of him, pleasant and easy to take.

I saw him looking at the water cooler.

'Can I offer you some iced water?'

'I'd like that, thanks.'

He held the glass in his right hand and took the contents down at one grateful draught. Immediately, beads of perspiration appeared on his forehead. He mopped at his face with a handkerchief that was as white as any television commercial.

'The matter about which I am here, Mr. Preston, is one of the greatest delicacy.

I inclined my head. The words may

vary, but practically everyone who ever comes into my office starts off with something of the kind.

'I have been sent to you because our enquiries show that you are the leading man in your field in this area. I may say that you have been checked very thoroughly before a decision was reached to entrust this matter to you.'

Mr. Hillier didn't mean to be pompous, it just came out that way. The bit about his being sent was intriguing. Who sent him?

'I think I can promise absolute reliability, Mr. Hillier. Not results. I've been too long in this business to guarantee results, but we'll do our best and it's a fairly good best, as my charges should convince you.'

He didn't smile, just sat listening intently.

'Oh, yes, I'm aware that your prices are high. However, the man I represent has never been one to quibble about that sort of thing.' He looked at the door. 'Is there any possibility of our being overheard?'

'None. That door is three inches thick.'

'Good. Now, Mr. Preston, I propose to give you an outline of the problem, no names mentioned. If it seems to be something you might undertake with success, I'll tell you more. If not, we need waste no more of each other's time. Would that seem reasonable?'

'Fair enough.'

I helped myself to an Old Favourite, held the pack out to Hillier, who declined. The smoke tasted dry and bitter in my mouth.

'There is a prominent man involved, a man with extensive business interests. At the moment there are some very intricate manoeuvres in progress concerning these interests, which stand to profit this man to a considerable extent. These negotiations have not yet reached the boardroom discussion level, but are still in the stage of after-dinner talks. I'm sure you grasp the picture.'

I grasped the picture. Two or three men exchanging casual remarks which could be the preliminary to a deal involving hundreds of thousands of dollars, maybe millions.

'I need hardly say that any publicity unfavourable to this man could damage these negotiations irreparably.'

I nodded again. It was my only contribution so far. I wished Mr. Hillier would either get down to business or go away and let me head for the Beach end.

'At this very trying time a young woman has approached this man. She claims to be pregnant and states that he is the father of her unborn child. There is no truth in it whatsoever, but it could be an embarrassment.'

'I see. And you want me to talk her out of it?'

'We want her stopped. How you do it is your affair. No questions will be asked.'

This was a very old situation indeed. Except for the bit about the merger or whatever it was, this story went back to where the principals had to talk in Sanskrit. Maybe the guy was responsible for the girl's condition and maybe not, it wouldn't make any material difference to the spot he was in right now.

'There are medical tests for this kind of thing, you know,' I said.

'Even the doctors will tell you they're not one hundred per cent reliable. In any case, none would be possible for several months, by which time it could well be too late to salvage the negotiations.'

That was true enough.

'What made the girl pick on this particular man? Does he know her?'

'No. There are two alternatives. One is that she found herself in this condition and decided to attempt blackmail on one of the leading business figures in the State, in which case my superior was selected by chance.' He looked at my face to see what I thought of that one.

I said:

'And the other?'

'The other is that certain other people have learned of my superior's vulnerability at this time, and are using the girl to advance their own interests at his expense.'

That sounded a little far-fetched, but I've come across some pretty odd transactions carried on in the fair name of business.

'How about lawyers? Have you consulted any?'

'Absolutely not. There can be no question of any legal proceedings. By the time his innocence was established, the damage would have been done.'

He had me there, too. I began to see that Mr. X was indeed on the spot. It was a little early for sympathy. It's been known for these cases to be proven in the girl's favour before now. Could be the guy was responsible at that, whatever he'd told the upright Mr. Hillier.

'What am I supposed to do, buy the girl off?'

He shook his head emphatically.

'Not one dollar. Not a red cent. We would like you to investigate the girl. Find out about her background, her associates. See if you can discover anyone who may have prompted her to this blackmail. When you find who's behind her, we can consider further what to do.'

'And if I don't find anyone?'

He smirked.

'We think there's a fair chance that you will.'

I didn't go for it, not altogether. It sounded too much like the big tycoon using vast resources to put the squeeze on some poor kid who'd been unlucky. But it was early to judge. I'd have to see the girl first. The poor kid of my imagination might turn out to be a hard-faced blonde with a long history of call-girl activities. Hillier didn't rush me, he just sat there quietly while I thought about what he'd been saying.

'O.K. I'll give it a try. Tell me the rest.'

He smiled pleasantly. He had nice white, even teeth. Dean Hillier wasn't exactly a man the women would run from screaming. With my bad old mind working the way it always does, I wondered for a brief second whether Mr. Hillier was using the confidential information he held as a means to putting the bite on his boss. It wouldn't be hard for him to find a girl to help out. I dismissed the thought as quickly as it came. He took a flat Morocco wallet from the inside pocket of his jacket. With his thumb and first finger he removed a small white card and passed it to me. It said, 'Dean Willman Hillier — Personal Assistant to the President.' In the top left-hand corner of the card was the legend — 'The Van Huizen Corporation.'

'Van Huizen? *The* Van Huizen?' I asked.

'Quite so.'

Mr. Hillier hadn't exaggerated one little bit. The Van Huizen Corporation was among the top few chemical concerns in the world. The reigning President, Benedict Van Huizen, was grandson of the founder, and his personal fortune amounted to anybody's guess.

'If I've followed you correctly, Mr. Hillier, what you've been telling me must concern Benedict Van Huizen himself.'

'You are absolutely correct in that assumption.'

'How's for one or two questions?'

'Certainly,' he replied.

'Your boss is an important man, very important. How come you've brought this thing to me instead of one of the big outfits?'

He smiled easily.

'For one thing, there is the security angle. Now I don't say there's any suggestion that our business would be mishandled elsewhere. I'm sure the larger organizations would be every bit as trustworthy as yourself. But their very size makes them unsuitable. They have to have filing systems, reports made out and so forth. It's no use having a secret, Mr. Preston, if you're going to confide in too many people. Ask anyone connected with security matters during World War II.'

He had me there. I nodded reluctantly.

'Matter of fact, I had a little something to do with that myself. I can't pretend I don't know what you mean.'

'Exactly. Then there's the time factor. This girl has appeared from nowhere. Our first word from her was on Saturday last. She has only given my employer until tomorrow to meet her demands.'

'Which are?'

'Twenty thousand dollars to be deposited in her name at a certain bank. A formal legal agreement to pay her one hundred dollars a week for life.'

I pursed my lips and let out a soft whistle. It made my visitor uncomfortable. People around the Corporation evidently did not behave the way I did.

'Nice round figures,' I said. 'If I've only got until tomorrow, I'd better cry off. You don't need a private investigator. But I know where to contact one or two magicians, if that'll help.'

His smile was as weak as the gag.

'That won't be necessary, I'm sure. Tomorrow is the lady's deadline at the moment, but once she feels things are moving, she'll probably be persuaded easily enough to extend the time limit.' He took out the startling white handkerchief again and did some more mopping. 'The lady is expecting to meet Mr. Van Huizen's personal representative this evening. You will be the man she meets.'

'Fine. It'll save a lot of trouble if I just club her to death and dump her in the desert, won't it?'

'I know that is supposed to be a joke, Mr. Preston, but I'd like to make it quite clear to you that before our interview this morning was decided upon, every possible alternative solution was considered. Every one.' He waited until that part soaked in, then, 'Unfortunately, if anything happens to the girl, a complete case history will be on the District Attorney's desk the following morning.'

'I see.'

I didn't care for the calm way Mr. Smooth Hillier sat there, practically telling me he'd considered hiring torpedoes to get rid of the inconvenient Miss Whoever-she-was. Everything about this deal up to now put me four-square in the girl's corner. And with my experience that was a mite ridiculous.

'What's this girl's name?'

'Cheryl Vickers. She has an apartment. The address is Fourteen A, 1227 Alamedo Avenue.'

He spoke slowly enough for me to write it on a nice clean sheet of paper. It wasn't necessary, the details were stamped firmly in my mind. But there's one thing I learned a long time ago in this business. The customers don't think you're paying the proper attention to their troubles if you don't write things down occasionally.

'Description?'

He coughed slightly.

'Well, of course, I've never seen the lady, but I understand she's of medium

13

height, about twenty-four years old, and has flaming red hair.'

I didn't ask him who he understood these things from.

'Now, what's the deal about tonight?' I demanded.

'Mr. Van Huizen has promised the girl he'll send his personal representative to meet her. Nine o'clock in the bar at the Club Rendezvous. Our man will wear a white carnation.'

'I'm not much for flowers — ' I protested, but he ignored me.

'The girl Vickers will make herself known to you. After that, the way in which you proceed will be entirely at your discretion.'

I was slightly ruffled by Hillier's calm assurance.

'What's to prevent me teaming up with the redhead and putting the bite on the Corporation for a vice-presidency or something?'

I might as well have saved my breath.

'The Corporation trusts you implicitly, Mr. Preston.' He spread his hands wide. 'Your character, your record, everything about your past history indicates an honest man.'

I had to make a dent in this guy somewhere. He'd got every angle covered, every route checked. He'd have made a swell bank stick-up organiser.

'Now let me ask you something a little nearer home,' I said. 'Your business card says you're Van Huizen's personal assistant. I guess it has to be very personal, doesn't it, for him to take you into his confidence over a thing like this?'

He sat there for a moment, thinking over the question, trying to decide whether the accent on the word 'personal' could be interpreted a certain way.

'I don't propose to explain myself to you, Mr. Preston. Here,' he dug into the wallet again and produced a folded piece of notepaper.

I smoothed it out. It was memorandum paper, the kind used for inter-office notes in big business concerns. The words 'Van Huizen Corporation' were heavily embossed as a centre heading. A little box on the left-hand side contained one word, 'President'. On the right was another box with the printed word 'To'. After that was added in ink simply 'Dean'. The note itself was also hand-written, in a firm, confident style, the letters sloping slightly to the right. It said:

'Re our conversation this morning I have decided to engage the man P. whom you recommend for the work. He will report to me through you, and I rely on you for up-to-the-minute information. Draw on the private account for whatever you need.

Van Huizen.'

'Does that satisfy you, Mr. Preston?'

'I guess it does. O.K. for me to keep the note?'

He hesitated, then

'Well, I don't see why not. One thing, though. If Mr. Van Huizen should by any chance query any of the expenditure incurred, I'd like the note back so that I can remind him of what he said.'

'Of course. I think that about does it. I usually charge a retainer — '

More business with the wallet. Then

there was a pink cheque lying on the table. It was made out to me, dated that day, and signed 'Dean W. Hillier'. In the vital space was written 'Five Hundred Dollars'. The cheque was a specially printed one for the Corporation, and was stamped 'Private Account — President'.

'Is the sum satisfactory?' enquired Hillier.

'Very. Of course, I shall charge expenses.'

'That is understood.'

He got up from the chair.

'After you have seen the girl this evening, I shall be at Mr. Van Huizen's residence from about ten onwards. You could telephone me there, or if there was anything really important, you could come out and report personally.'

I digested that.

'Come out there?' I queried. 'Suppose I run into Mrs. Van Huizen. Won't she want to know why a stranger is calling that late at night?'

'She'll know why you're calling. Mrs. Van Huizen is entirely aware of every detail of this business.'

Well, that one floored me. Hillier had led on points from the first round, but to save a great big sucker punch like that for the tenth was asking too much of my poor brain on a hot morning.

I showed him out and we shook hands again. I liked him. I went back and sat behind the desk, looked at the chair he'd just vacated. Went back over the conversation, remembering his every expression. He'd been ready with an answer to everything I'd asked, and I liked him. Dean Hillier was the efficient executive down to his manicured finger-nails. If he was an example of the guys running things over at V.H.C., I'd better get some of my money invested in that direction. Not that I really thought I could do much with Cheryl Vickers. This particular tale had been told too often before, and the trouble was the guy on the end of the hook had two alternatives when you boiled it right down. He could pay or he could pay. Anyway, it was kind of early in the day to throw in the towel. I pulled the telephone towards me and thumbed through the directory. Then I dialled a number. There was some burring and a cheerful girl's voice said,

'Good morning. Van Huizen Corporation.'

'I want to talk with Mr. Hillier, please. Dean Willman Hillier.'

'Just a moment.'

Some clicking, and another girl, still cheerful, but in a lower key.

'Mr. Dean Hillier's office.'

'I'd like to speak with him, please. This is — ' I screwed the cheque around on the desk ' — this is the United California Trust Bank. I have a cheque here I would like Mr. Hillier to confirm.'

'I'm sorry, sir, Mr. Hillier is not here at present.'

'Well, this is rather urgent. Have you a number where I could reach him, please?'

'Just a moment, I'll see.'

She went off the line. Through the window I could make out in the distance the white sails of a small yacht. What was I doing sitting here while those guys were out there splashing around and living it up?

'Hallo? Oh, yes. I have found the

19

number where Mr. Hillier might be reached. Will you take it down?'

'Thank you.'

She read out the number slowly and I repeated it carefully back, one numeral at a time. I thanked her again and hung up. I hadn't needed to write the number down. It was the same as the one printed on the telephone I was holding. My visitor had been the genuine article.

According to my strap-watch, it was eleven-forty-five in the forenoon. On my desk was a cheque for five hundred dollars. That seemed to add up to a fair return for a fair morning's work. I pushed the buzzer and ten seconds later Florence Digby came into the room. Florence had been with me almost three years. I'd been working for ten-dollar fees in a fourth-floor room downtown when she first appeared. Now I was in a three-room suite on the second floor, uptown, and the expensive furniture was paid for. She just moved right in, with her typewriter, headed notepaper, filing system, that kind of stuff. I'd never been much for office routine, but she changed all that, and me with it. I hadn't been much for working myself to death either, but somehow that woman kept me at it. It seemed to pay off, at that. My credit was good anywhere in the State, and the bank manager always said 'Good morning' when he saw me. I always like to tell myself that natural talent would have brought me these things in the end, but there was an insistent connection between my move up in the world and Florence Digby that I couldn't always deny.

'Yes, Mr. Preston?'

'Miss Digby, we have a client,' I waved the cheque. 'Will you kindly deposit this?'

'Certainly, Mr. Preston.'

She took the slip of paper and read it.

'H'm. A very reputable client, Mr. Preston. Not a man who'd have engaged anyone from River Street.'

I didn't want to quarrel with the Digby today.

'You're absolutely right. River Street is behind us. Nowadays a man has to have a front.'

She unbent enough to manage a small smile. Florence must have been close to

21

forty-five years old, but every now and then you got an idea of what a dish she must have been a few years back.

'It's very hot today. What are you doing at the moment?'

'Just clearing up your report on the Barnett matter. Why?'

'I was thinking. Nothing will break on that till Friday at least. This new caper,' I pointed at the cheque, 'that starts tonight. What do you say we close up and take the afternoon off?'

She looked longingly out of the window.

'I — I don't know. Maybe something will — '

'Now look. No matter what comes in, I'm already tied up. So let's get out of this oven before we roast right through, huh?'

'Well, it certainly would be nice. Just for once.'

'Fine.'

I started to get up, reaching for my coat.

'I'll just bring in those Barnett papers for you to check, and then we can leave.'

I didn't argue with her. I checked the

file, gave her my O.K. and we locked up for the day. I dropped her off close to the bank and headed back to Parkside. In my bum days I sometimes used to tell myself I'd wind up with an address at the Parkside Towers, but I never really believed it. Now, here I was. It cost plenty, but a guy with no responsibilities has a right to a little comfort, and comfort is the speciality of the house at Parkside. There is an unseen army that moves into the apartment when I leave in the morning and cleans up. The service is smooth, like a well-oiled watch movement, and it will be a long time before I can take all the luxury for granted. Maybe it does a man good to have memories like I have of River Street, to make him appreciate the things money can buy.

It was no day for lunch. I tried a salad sandwich alongside a glass of iced beer in a joint down by the shore. The food had all the attraction of chewed paper, but the beer was headed in the right direction. Later I sat around on the rocks, watching the blue water transform itself into a white froth against the shore line, then gently sliding back. It must have been my wet feet that woke me. My watch said it was close to five o'clock, and the sea had inched up some in the meantime. Both my feet were now firmly planted in the white spray. Another hour and I'd have been surrounded. I moved out of there fast. One or two people looked curiously at the wet marks I made as I headed for the spot I'd left the car. They didn't improve my feelings any.

I went home and climbed under a shower. The sleep hadn't done me any harm. A man feeling as good as I felt could have a lot worse prospect for the evening than meeting a mysterious redhead at a place like the Club Rendezvous. I loafed around the apartment till almost eight o'clock. Then I put on a fresh linen suit and checked my billfold. There were three twenties, two tens and some dollar bills. That ought to be enough for what was on the programme. After some hesitation I took the .38 along as well. You never can tell how things will turn out when you start off on what looks like a harmless errand.

The evening was hot and still. People were starting to appear in their glad rags. I dropped the heap in the parking lot. The Club Rendezvous was the latest business venture of gambler Frank Kalmus. It had been open about three months now and was the current place to go. Tricked out in Palm Beach style, the place featured soft lighting and soft-footed waiters. There was a four-piece band that dreamed up soft rhythms, and maybe a soft-voiced girl who'd sing a number or two. Slow and easy was the keynote of the Rendezvous. Naturally the customers paid in hard cash, but the thing was done so you'd hardly notice the pain. I stood on the veranda and looked through an open window. I could see the restaurant and part of the bar. No redhead as yet. Inside a soft, round girl was glad to supply the white carnation I needed. I gave her ten and got a five in return, but she had such a nice smile and so much of what goes with it that I found myself walking into the bar before the price registered. The bar was long and set close to the wall. It was done in a dove-grey plastic that matched the thick carpeting. I ordered Scotch on the rocks and watched the barman to see which bottle he selected. His hand came out with the bottle in.

'Uh-uh,' I negatived.

He looked up and caught my eye in the wall mirror. Then he pushed the bottle back into place, and ran his eye along. He pointed with his stubby forefinger at another collector's item.

'Fine. Make it a big one.'

He made it a big one, dropped pieces of cracked ice into the mellow liquid with a pair of silver tongs.

'Every guest has his own particular brand, sir.'

'Sure.'

He gave my five dollar bill some pretty rough treatment and set a neat pile of small nickel coins in front of me. Now I could make a 'phone call. I was beginning to wonder whether it wouldn't have been smarter for me to do my drinking somewhere else, and arrive at the Rendezvous at one minute to nine. I parked on a tall stool at the end of the bar furthest from the entrance giving the white carnation plenty of advertising. There were a couple of other solitary drinkers on view, and a middle-aged man and woman who sat talking quietly in a corner. I had a clear view into the restaurant where business was getting brisk. The waiters moved silently around and the haunting sweetness of a tenor saxophone drifted over the air. At a corner table I noticed Eddie Newman sitting with a slim, sun-tanned woman. I'll try that again. First I noticed the woman, Eddie was way down the field. She wore a pale lemon dinner gown, cut high in the front and low at the back. Her shoulders and back were a rich brown colour which contrasted well with the colour of the material. Her face was oval-shaped with high cheek-bones, and the only make-up on it was lipstick. She had dark eyes and they were all for Eddie Newman. The watch on her slim wrist was gold, she wasn't a girl who'd wear any imitation stuff. Her long fingers moved restlessly at the side of the frosted glass which stood before her on the snowy

27

tablecloth. To look at them you'd think these two had forgotten there was anyone else in the place.

I often wondered how Eddie did it. Strictly speaking, I guess he was on his working time. He operates as number two man for Frank Kalmus, and had been acting as manager of the club since it opened. Not that he was really a gambler himself, you might say he kind of graduated into it. He was really a fighter, light heavy, and pretty damned good a few years back. I'd seen him in the Golden Gloves stuff before he went pro. and there wasn't a cleaner hitter nor a daintier man on his feet than Ed Newman. It used to be Neumann, but when the money boys took him over they figured the Neumann tag was no good for the big time, so enter Mr. Newman. Eddie was a little over thirty now, and five feet ten inches of very well-cared-for muscle. I've nothing to be ashamed of with my shirt off, but Ed's one of those guys who make all the other fellows feel under-nourished. He has dark, crinkly hair and is not a bad-looking proposition, including the slightly bent nose which was a memento from one night at the Garden with a character known as Battling Bert McGinty. In fact, it was that particular fight that first made me wonder about Ed. He was at his peak then, and this McGinty was nothing but a beer-swilling bar-fighter. I had fifty on Ed, and it was hard to persuade anyone to accept it, the result was such a certainty. But Ed stopped one in the fifth, and that moved McGinty up to contender status. The smart money made a pile and a lot of ordinary joes learned a lesson. I saw the newsreel of that fight, and it was an insult to the game. Fifty bucks was a lot of money to me in those days, and I took a special interest in Mr. Newman's progress from there on. He had about a dozen more fights, losing three decisions that cost me nothing, then retired. He was practically unmarked, worth a fair amount of money, and was marked O.K. by the crooks who'd been telling him what to do. He didn't have such a good name with the legions of fight fans, but who cared for their opinion? They were only the suckers who filled the stadium and provided the cash that made the set-ups possible. And now here he was, in a white tuxedo with a crimson bow-tie, very much occupied with the woman at his side. He said something, and she laughed. The red lips parted and the subdued table light sparkled on a row of strong, even teeth. She made all the other women in the place look like a glass of beer that's been standing in a warm room.

It was some little time before I registered the fact that someone was taking a particular interest in these two. Several of the men on view had admired the girl, naturally, but I came to realise that the fat man sitting alone by the restaurant entrance hadn't taken his eyes off the pair. He looked out of place in his creased, badly-fitting blue suit. He was George Porter, a man I hate to admit was in my own line of business. The kind of P.I. who gets the rest of us a bad name. Close to fifty, he'd been a cop once, busted three years before for being on the take. Now he'd turn his hand to anything anybody wanted doing. Things people wouldn't dare take to the police, and respectable agencies wouldn't handle. Nothing was too low for our George. I wondered idly what he was up to.

It was past nine now and still no sign of the redhead. I bought another drink, and sat there watching the place fill up. Lots of people on vacation turn up in Monkton City for an evening out from the resorts along the coast. Most of the faces were unfamiliar, though here and there I could pick out the ones who hadn't come to the Rendezvous for the soft music. Frank Kalmus wasn't the man to speculate all this money on a strictly dine-and-dance joint. Up the narrow white staircase was a place reserved for the personal guests of the proprietor. What that meant was that there were tables covered in green baize where you could roll the dice or bet on a spinning wheel, or even risk a try at blackjack. If, that is, your roll was thick enough. Now and again someone would elbow his way through the mob in the bar, exchange a few words with the waiter who hovered unobtrusively at the bottom of the stairs, then go on up. The waiter was dressed like a waiter, but he hadn't learned his method of speaking from hovering over dinner-jackets and low-cut gowns. The tight lips and the clipped words from the side of his mouth were the graduation diplomas of the line-up and the exercise yard.

At nine-thirty I got off my stool and took a walk around outside. I looked in every window to see if I could spot my redhead, and even tried to walk with my left shoulder stuck forward so everyone could see the white bloom at the lapel. No bids. The only development was that the stool was now occupied by an enormous woman who flowed all over it every which way. I fought my way to the bar and finally managed to get a drink, with which I retreated to the only empty spot in the place, by the side wall. At ten-fifteen I was wedged solidly in place by a large party of not-so-young people who were all a little drunk, and passed the time trying to out-shout and out-laugh each other. It seemed to me that even for five hundred dollars I'd done enough for one evening. The redhead was not going to show. I didn't know Miss Cheryl Vickers and I didn't particularly want to, but this I knew. A dame who was trying to pull the kind of stunt she was engaged on, would not fail to appear for an appointment which might turn out to be worth twenty grand and a hundred a week for life. I was reasonably sure that if we were going to make contact, it would not be at the Club Rendezvous that night. I parked my empty glass, managed to plant my elbow in the ribs of a thin woman who'd kicked me about eight times in the last ten minutes, and headed for the fresh air. I didn't see Ed Newman or his girl as I left.

Alamedo Avenue was a fifteen-minute ride and several tax brackets away from the place I'd just left. I coasted along checking the numbers on the buildings. When they were high in the eleven hundreds, I pulled into the kerb and got out. The Avenue was close to the business section of town and there were several apartment buildings for bachelor guys and girls where the rent measured up to the accommodation provided. Two rooms and bath and no noise after midnight, just the thing for young people just getting started who needed to be close to the job. 1227 stood back from the street and was slightly more impressive than some of the numbers I'd passed. There was a paved forecourt with raised beds of flowers set around the drive-in. It was seven storeys up to the top and many of the windows showed lights. The entrance was small and economical on the lighting. No one was around when I walked past the elevators and headed for the stairs.

Fourteen A was on the second floor, the third door along a corridor that led off at right angles from the stairs. There was a little name-plate with a white card set on the wall, but no name on it. I tried the buzzer, waited a minute or two, then tried again. For five hundred dollars I figure the customer is entitled to a little extra service. Slipping a small bunch of keys from my pocket, I tried two without success, but the third turned confidently to the left and the door moved inwards.

The strong moon-light through the open window showed me enough to find the switch. I snapped it down and found myself in a small room. Comfortable enough, but somehow impersonal. You couldn't have said whether it belonged to a man or a woman. I hoped briefly that Hillier hadn't steered me to the wrong address. A door led off to the right. It stood open. I crossed and looked into the bed-room. There was a girl lying on the bed. The auburn hair spread richly out around her head as it rested on the pillow. The heart-shaped face was beautiful, relaxed and almost smiling. She was wearing a skimpy sun-top bra and very brief shorts. Her long, slim legs were hanging slightly over the edge of the bed. There was a black hole under the left breast, which had bled hardly at all. Cheryl Vickers was all through blackmailing anybody. Whoever had killed her knew what he was doing. The bullet had been planted in exactly the right spot. She would have died instantly, almost without realising what was happening, which would account for the calm on her face. It was my first and only meeting with her, and I was angry. Waste always makes me that way, and it was a waste for this young, lovely girl to be cold and dead. There was no signs of a struggle, but I was only looking from habit. This girl hadn't been expecting any trouble. She'd been standing talking to somebody, and the somebody had stood, probably smiling back, and rested a heavy calibre gun against her heart and pulled the trigger, once. Just once. No panic, no squeezing away until the gun was half empty. Whoever it was hadn't acted in a blind rage, or on impulse. I knew it would be a waste of time checking the apartment. The killer would have taken away anything which might help those interested in finding out who he was. So I checked just the same. No papers, no photographs. Whoever the late Miss Vickers was, or had been, the law would have a swell time finding out. Of course, if she'd ever been in any trouble before, Criminal Identification would place her prints in no seconds flat. She didn't look a particularly hardened criminal to me, but the last girl I thought that about knifed her double-crossing boy friend in the stomach, then sat smoking while he crawled about the floor, dying.

I checked an ashtray and all that told me was that the girl smoked. Then I picked up the partly-burned paper match that rested among the stubs. The red printing on the side said, ' — ATE'S GRILL'. It didn't mean a thing to me. I slipped the match in my jacket pocket. Then I spent ten minutes or so wiping everything I'd touched when I first arrived. It was a pity that by covering my own tracks I was also making life easier for the killer, who may have left some trace behind. I moved back to the bedroom for a last look at Cheryl Vickers. It wasn't evident at first glance that she was dead. She could have just laid down for a rest. I had an impulse to go and lift her feet further on to the bed. It didn't seem right for them to be hanging that way. But the way she was may provide some kind of lead to the scientific boys in the Department when they finally caught up with this. I didn't have a hat I could take off, and I felt I had to do something about her, so I muttered, 'So long, Cheryl,' and headed out. My elbow knocked up the light switch, and I'm not going to say I wasn't glad to get out of Apartment Fourteen A.

I went back to the car and took a ride down to Sam's. There I ordered a triple decker and beer. At a corner table I set to work on the sandwich and did some thinking. I didn't care for some of the thoughts. It was now eleven-thirty, and kind of late to be telephoning the Van Huizen house. They might be early sleepers for all I knew. Then I thought about Cheryl Vickers, and counted out my small change. The phone at the other end was picked up at once. A man said:

'This is the Van Huizen house.'

His tone was guarded. So guarded you'd think he was the look-out for a bookie parlour.

'I'd like to talk with Mr. Van Huizen or Mr. Hillier,' I said.

There was a slight scraping noise, as though the man at the other end had put his hand over the mouthpiece. I waited a while, then —

'Who is that speaking, please?'

'The name is Mark Preston,' I told him.

More scraping and another wait. The same voice again.

'Could you come out here right away, Mr. Preston?'

'Now? But I'm in Monkton City. It'll take best part of an hour to get there. Do you know what time it is?'

'I have a watch, Mr. Preston. We'll expect you around twelve-thirty.'

'Look, what is this — ?' I began, then I stopped. I was talking into a dead phone.

Fine thing. If Van Huizen or anybody else thought I was going for a drive along the shore just for the fun of it, they could have another think. I jammed the telephone back on the hook and drove away from Sam's. I knew where there was an all-night gas station that would fill up my tank for the trip.

2

The small white board had an arrow point at one end. The legend read, 'Van Huizen', and the letters looked black in the car headlights. I swung off left and drove along the half-mile or so of curving driveway. At the end was an abrupt turn to the right and there was the house. The moon was strong, but it didn't help make the place look any prettier. It was an ugly, rambling structure. If memory served me, the original Van Huizen knew more about paints and chemicals than anyone else in the field, and less about anything else than the average Mongolian bandit. I imagined that by daylight the place would be an eyesore, but under the soft radiance of the moon it was only repulsive. There were lights on in several of the downstairs rooms. I could see where three or four other cars were parked in front of the house, so I pulled in beside the nearest, a cream sedan that was less than a mile long.

The front door was of heavy oak, bound with brass strips, and it was open. I looked around for a way to announce my arrival, found an old-fashioned bell-pull and tugged. There was a faint tinkle somewhere in the distance. I could hear voices coming from one of the rooms on the right-hand side of the hall. I peeked in at a window, but the heavy drapes blotted out any view.

'Just hold it right there.'

I froze in a half-bent position. The voice was behind me. Something was pressed against the nape of my neck. It was cold and hard. Then a hand come patting around my pockets, found the .38. The man grunted with satisfaction, hauled out the weapon. The coldness moved away.

'Let's step into the house. Nice and easy.'

I went into the hall. My new friend pushed past me and I got a look at a middle-aged man with tired eyes and a disillusioned face. Even without the Police Special which was aimed at my stomach I'd have known him. Cop. He motioned me towards a door, pushing it open with his foot. There were others inside, big men with hard faces, lines of suspicion etched deeply.

'I found this guy nosing around outside.'

They looked at me without particular interest.

'Who are you?'

The taller of the two was in his late fifties. His pants were pressed and he even had a shoe-shine. It was he who spoke.

'I'm Preston. I'm expected here.'

'Yeah.'

My dancing partner felt he was being cheated.

'How about this? He packs it in a side pocket.'

Proudly, he displayed my .38. The tall man showed slightly more animation.

'Got a licence?'

'Sure.'

I started to dive into my pocket, but he waved me down.

'O.K., O.K.' Turning to the arresting officer, he said, 'Get back outside and keep awake, will you?'

The guy looked slightly sheepish. As he walked past me I tapped him on the arm, pointing to the gun. He snorted and handed it over. The tall one looked over my shoulder and said,

'This the guy?'

'Yes.'

It was Dean Hillier's voice. He was huddled up in a chair behind the door which was why I hadn't seen him before. He didn't look half the man he'd been twelve hours earlier. His collar was rumpled and he was white-faced. An empty glass stood close by his trembling hand. All in all, he looked like hell.

'All right, Preston. Let's have the story.'

These guys were the law. Hillier looked like bad news. Maybe somebody had seen me in Cheryl's apartment, or I was tied in somehow. This interview could mean I was in trouble, kingsize.

'Story?' I looked baffled. 'Who are you, anyway?'

The shorter man sighed. The other one said,

'I'm Harrigan, County Sheriff's Office.

This is my deputy, Dunphy.'

Dunphy bared his teeth at me. They weren't good enough for that kind of advertising. Whatever these characters wanted, it wasn't my blood. Cheryl Vickers was city business, and the county men wouldn't be involved.

'I don't get it,' I remarked.

'Look, Preston, don't be hard to get along with,' sighed Harrigan. 'You don't want to resist arrest, do you?'

Dunphy looked quite cheerful at the prospect of some action.

'If you mean do I want four or five of your mugs kicking my ribs in, the answer is no.'

'So we understand each other. What are you doing here?' demanded Harrigan.

'I was told to come. I telephoned about an hour ago.'

'Sure. It was Dunphy you talked to. Now just tell us where you figure, what your business is, that's all.'

'I'm a private investigator. I got a licence for that, too, if you want to see it.' I went into my routine, but he shook his head. 'I have business with Mr. Van

Huizen. He's a client of mine and I don't have to discuss professional business.'

'We'll see about that. Mr. Hillier over there, he's Van Huizen's personal assistant or some such. How's for him to give the O.K. for you to spill?'

I shook my head.

'No deal. Hillier engaged me, sure, but it was on his boss's instructions. Seems to me the boss ought to decide whether I talk or not.'

'You want to see Mr. Van Huizen?'

'If he's available, certainly.'

Harrigan turned to the deputy.

'Tom, take *Mr.* Preston to see *Mr.* Van Huizen.'

Dunphy leered again and beckoned with his finger. I followed him out of the room, across the hall to a pair of closed doors. He led me inside. A uniformed cop rose from a chair. It was a large, comfortable room. The walls were lined with row after row of books. The furniture was heavy with leather coverings. In one corner stood a large desk, leather-topped, with old-fashioned silver ink-stand and a silver sand-shaker. Seated behind it was the man I'd come to see. He was in his late forties, dressed in a white tuxedo jacket with black bow-tie. His left hand rested on the desk next to a crystal glass whisky decanter. The decanter was almost empty. The black hair on his head was thinning. The rest of his face was a red horror. I grimaced. At my side the deputy chuckled.

'Pretty, ain't he?'

'How'd he get like that?'

What I meant was I couldn't make out how he died. There was too much mess.

'Stuck a .45 calibre revolver in his mouth pointing upwards. Then pulled the trigger.'

It was a chilling thought. The sweat on my forehead was cold and clammy.

'Let's get back.' Dunphy didn't sound so confident now. A few seconds looking at the late Van Huizen would have had that effect on anybody.

Neither Harrigan nor Hillier had moved when we returned.

'I can tell by your face you've seen him,' said Harrigan. 'Help yourself to a drink, then we'll talk.'

I nodded. There was an assortment of bottles in view in an open cabinet. Three fingers of brandy hit the spot.

'I have an office in Monkton City. This morning he telephoned.' I pointed to Hillier and started on the tale.

Harrigan and Dunphy threw questions as I went along. At one point Hillier started to interrupt, but they shut him up fast. What they wanted was to hear me tell it. Presumably they'd heard it all from Hillier already and were just checking.

'So you went to the club at nine?'

'A little before.'

'What time did the dame show?'

'She didn't.'

'She what?'

'She didn't show.'

Dunphy said,

'What you giving us, Preston? This is a shakedown, the sucker turns up and the blackmailer doesn't?'

'That's right. She didn't come.'

They were both annoyed about it. It was screwy. I was available for questioning, and that made it my fault. They were right, it did smell. I couldn't very well say that Cheryl hadn't arrived because somebody killed her before she got started.

'Look, why don't you guys get wise? I got no reason to tell you the tale. If you don't believe me, ask her, ask the girl.'

'Don't tell us our business, Preston. We'll get around to her when we're good and ready. This suicide is County business. We can ask for the girl as a material witness when we're establishing motive,' said Harrigan.

'That's right,' agreed his deputy. 'We don't want no city guys busting into this deal. This is right off limits for them.'

I sat there and fumed. The suicide of a wealthy industrialist would make the front pages for sure. These two dumb characters were going to work out the whole deal ironclad, and no other law officers were going to muscle in on the publicity. They couldn't just go into Monkton and grab the girl. The proper thing to do was contact the city police and ask them to pick her up, but that might involve a little of the credit for the investigation going to the wrong quarter. Meantime, Cheryl's body went undiscovered, and the fact that it was my fault as much as theirs didn't make me feel any better.

'What makes you so sure it was suicide?' I asked innocently.

'Everything checks. Van Huizen got home around ten. The butler says he was very bad-tempered and excited. He was also very drunk. He told the butler to go to bed and to make sure he wasn't disturbed. Then he went into the library. At ten-thirty there was this shot. The butler went in and found him the way you saw him. Then Hillier arrived a few minutes later, and sent for us.'

'Not a doctor?'

'Be your age, Preston. You've been in there. What would you imagine a doctor could do?'

'Unless it was a witch-doctor.' It was Dunphy's idea of a joke.

Harrigan gave him a ferocious glare.

'All right, suppose it was suicide,' I jumped in. 'Why would he do it?'

'If I knew that, I wouldn't be here,'

snarled Harrigan. 'I'd be home in bed.'

I shrugged my shoulders.

'Well, anyway, I've told you all I can. It's getting kind of late. Any objection to my leaving now?'

Dunphy moved obtrusively towards the door.

'Yeah, I got a few objections,' he said.

'That's right. Sit down, Preston, and let me tell you something that nags at my poor old brain.'

I hesitated. I didn't think Deputy Dunphy would be much of a problem, he was too far out of condition. Then he put his hand casually inside his pocket and there was something there besides his hand. That made the difference. I went and sat down. Harrigan nodded with approval.

'Now you take Van Huizen. There's a smart man. There *was* a smart man,' he corrected himself. 'Big business, plenty of dough. Maybe he likes to fool around with the women. Where's the harm?'

I pushed an Old Favourite between my lips, and felt around for my cigarette lighter.

'Then you take Hillier, here,' he jerked a thumb towards the disconsolate figure of the secretary, who didn't seem to have moved since I arrived. 'There's another smart boy. Good brain, everything. Maybe he sometimes thinks he doesn't get a fair share of the gravy. And who's to blame him?'

I knew the street Harrigan was headed down. I'd passed that way myself ten minutes after I arrived at the house.

'Could be Hillier gets to hear that one of his boss's friends is in a little trouble. That kind of trouble. He sees a chance to earn a few extra bucks. Gives his boss some misleading advice, then contacts somebody like you to help out with the details. Maybe even takes you in as a partner.'

'Brilliant,' I said. 'And what's the value of this to Hillier and me? Who are we going to tell? His wife? She knows all about it already.'

'You say.' Harrigan pointed a finger at me. 'He says.' It was Hillier's turn. 'I ain't heard Mrs. Van Huizen say so yet.'

That was true.

'Where is the lady anyway? Having a breakdown?' I asked.

'If she is, she's not doing it here. She hasn't been home all evening.'

'Look, Harrigan,' I said impatiently, 'this whole thing is ridiculous. If Hillier wanted to shake Van Huizen down, he could have done it a dozen times a week. He has access to all the meetings, all the private papers, why should he get mixed up in a lousy little thing like us?'

'Who knows about people? Not me, and I've been on this job twenty years on and off.'

He'd got an idea in his head, and nothing I said was likely to shift it.

'So we wait around for the lady?'

'We do.'

I looked across at Hillier. He looked back in despair. I felt sorry for him. He'd been so brisk and confident at my office in the morning. That was before he'd seen his boss with his brains scrambled all over his face. Maybe he just wasn't cut out for this kind of situation. I turned back to the man from the County Sheriff's Office.

'When she gets here, if it turns out she

knows all about this deal, you'll see things a little differently, yes?'

He crossed one pressed trouser leg over the other.

'If Mrs. Van Huizen is aware of everything, it certainly won't go against you boys.'

'You realise that if you had the girl picked up, you could have us cleared in about five minutes flat?'

I only said it to annoy him. It annoyed him.

'Don't let me hear any more about that dame — ' he started.

The door opened and the man who'd shown me his gun came in.

'Car coming up the drive, chief.'

'All right. Outside.' When the door closed again he said, 'Well, maybe this is the little lady now.'

'Maybe it's the rest of our mob,' I answered, 'with tommy-guns and tear gas.'

'That's a joke,' said Dunphy, 'I can always tell.'

Hillier stood up suddenly. We all looked at him in surprise.

'If you don't mind, I'd like to be the one to break the news to Mrs. Van Huizen,' he said uncertainly. 'She's rather highly strung; a thing like this — '

'Sure. No objection,' replied Harrigan, 'but in here. You tell her in here, where I know what's going on.'

Hillier nodded dumbly. There was a mirror on the wall. He went over and made an effort to improve his appearance. He could do nothing about his face, where shock was written clear. There was the noise of a car door banging, silence, then the front door was closed. I could hear the tap-tapping of high heels across the hall, and a woman's voice softly humming a tune. We looked at each other, and silently agreed that none of us wanted Hillier's job. The door handle turned and she came into the room, stopping dead at sight of the four of us. A chin-chilla wrap was thrown around the brown shoulders, but otherwise she looked the same as when I saw her last. Marcia Van Huizen was the girl I'd seen with Eddie Newman at the Club Rendezvous.

'Dean, what's going on? Who are these people?'

She was very cool and unworried. The school back East where she'd learned those clipped tones had turned out the finished product when Marcia graduated. Hillier took a step towards her, raised a hand, then let it fall back to his side.

'Marcia, it's Ben. He — he's — ' He faltered. Her eyes never left his face. 'There's been an accident, Marcia. Ben's hurt.'

Her hand flew to her throat, and the voice was pitched half a tone higher.

'Hurt? Take me to him, Dean.'

'Marcia,' Hillier's screwed-up courage deserted him suddenly. He blurted out, 'Ben's dead.'

'Dead?'

There was disbelief in the whispered word. She looked at each of us in turn — Dunphy, me, Harrigan. She wanted one of us to say Hillier was wrong, that there'd been some mistake. I guess the others felt as uncomfortable as me. Harrigan cleared his throat.

'I'm afraid what Mr. Hillier says is true,

Mrs. Van Huizen. I'm very sorry.'

'Who are you?'

'We're police officers.'

She didn't give any sign that she'd heard him, but turned to Dean Hillier.

'I want to see him, Dean.'

'Marcia, I wouldn't go in there if I were you. I don't think . . . '

'Take me to him.' There was no arguing with the finality in her tone.

Hillier looked at Harrigan, who shrugged.

'If you insist. He's in the library.'

She turned and walked out, Hillier tagging along behind. When they'd gone, Dunphy ran a stubby finger round inside his collar.

'Whew.'

I knew what he meant. A little while passed, then we heard them coming back into the room. I went across and poured some brandy into a glass, with a suspicion of soda. Marcia walked in. Her face was drawn now, but there were no tears. She was under control, and with luck would be able to hold it that way. I handed her the glass which she held steadily enough. Then she drank the brandy in two quick nervous swallows, catching her breath slightly. She held the glass out for me to take.

'Thank you, Mr. — ?'

'Preston.'

'Thank you, Mr. Preston. May I have a cigarette, please?'

I held out my pack. Hillier was ahead of me with a silver case, but she ignored it, and took one of mine. I lit it for her. She nodded her thanks and went to a chair in the middle of the room.

'Who is in charge?'

'I am, ma'am. Harrigan is the name, County Sheriff's Office. This is Sergeant Dunphy.'

'Thank you. And you, Mr. Preston?'

'Preston was working for Ben. He's a private investigator.' This from Hillier.

Marcia flicked at her cigarette with a slim finger.

'Do you know who killed my husband, Mr. Harrigan?'

'Killed him?' Harrigan was puzzled. 'You're jumping to the wrong conclusion there, Mrs. Van Huizen. Your husband killed himself. This is a suicide matter.'

'Rubbish, Mr. Harrigan.' She said it quite calmly; they might have been discussing the weather. 'You walk into my house, a place you've never entered before. You look at the — ' she hesitated, ' — the body of a dead man, whom you didn't know, and decide that it was suicide.'

'All the facts — ' began Harrigan.

'Facts? I'll tell you some facts, policeman. Benedict Van Huizen was fond of life. He liked parties, company and excitement. He is — was a very wealthy man. One of the wealthiest in the United States. He was negotiating something which would have made him one of the richest men in the whole world. These are facts. Are you listening to me?'

Harrigan nodded. I found myself nodding, too. Marcia Van Huizen was one of those rare people. When she spoke, you listened.

'He had every reason to live. Why should he commit suicide? This was murder, Mr. Harrigan.'

Her tone was final. To do Harrigan credit, he didn't back down.

'I'm a professional investigator of crime. A wealthy man to me is no different to a working joe. I know a suicide when I see one. And while we're on facts, ma'am, maybe there's one you don't know.'

She looked at him levelly.

'Well?'

'I'm sorry to bring it up at a time like this, but your husband was having some trouble over — excuse me — another woman.'

I liked Harrigan better than at any time since I'd arrived. Marcia tossed her head.

'That little slut. I know all about her. What's the connection?'

I looked expressively at Harrigan, who ignored me.

'Well, I apologise, I didn't think you would know about her.' He floundered around, looking for something solid to grasp. He grasped the wrong thing, the way you always do in a hurry. 'It's possible that there's been some development there. The girl may have told your husband she was going to the newspapers or something.'

Harrigan had spent the whole night nursing his little theory that Cheryl tied in with Hillier, and possibly me. He hadn't bothered to think any further than that, coupled with the conviction that Van Huizen would have kept the thing from his wife. Now he was in trouble. Marcia considered what he'd been saying.

'And have you found anything out yet? Anything to confirm that?'

'Not yet, ma'am.' Harrigan looked imploringly at me. I was about to say something, but Hillier got there first.

'No, Marcia, Mr. Harrigan hasn't got very far at all yet. No further than thinking that I organised the blackmail, with some help from Preston here. He hasn't even made any attempt to have the girl apprehended.'

'Is this true, Mr. Harrigan?'

He swallowed hard.

'You see, ma'am — '

'Yes, I think I do.' She ground out the cigarette in a neat, decisive movement. 'I know a little about the political machinery in this area. It is undoubtedly your misfortune, Mr. Harrigan, that I haven't collapsed under this stress. You would have been very much better suited if I had. But I come from pioneer stock. First, I'll bury my dead. I'll tolerate no political chicanery in this matter. You have one hour to get some definite results with this girl. Now please leave this room. You may use the room next to the library. It has a telephone.'

For a moment I thought he was going to give her an argument. Then he nodded curtly and strode out. Dunphy was only inches behind. My hand was on the door handle when she said,

'Not you, Mr. Preston. I'd like to talk to you, please. Would you mind, Dean?'

'Of course not.'

Hillier walked to the door, turned around to say something, changed his mind, and was gone.

'Do sit down, Mr. Preston.'

'Could I have a drink?'

'Help yourself.'

I poured myself a generous helping. She had one, too. Now that the exchange with Harrigan was over signs of strain were beginning to show on her face. Tiny lines had appeared at the corners of her eyes and her forehead was creasing slightly. I took a chair opposite and admired the scenery. She'd thrown the wrap on the seat beside her, and I was able to get a grandstand view of the sunburn which had attracted my attention in the Club Rendezvous.

'Would it surprise you very much if I told you I had little faith in the police?' she queried.

'Not too much. Specially after the way you pushed Harrigan around.'

'Then you've an idea of what I want to talk to you about?'

I shook out one of my last remaining Old Favourites from the battered pack.

'You're going to ask me to find out who murdered your husband,' I said matter-of-factly.

'Well, will you do it?'

I thought it over.

'Look, Mrs. Van Huizen, I'm just a guy with a private licence. Harrigan and the rest of the County boys couldn't find anything to indicate this wasn't suicide. There'll be nothing in that library now to give me a lead of any kind, even if there was anything to be found in the first place.'

'I would be prepared to pay a great deal of money,' she said slowly.

'And stop waving your cheque-book in my face,' I told her irritably. 'There's a hundred guys will be glad to take this investigation on, and send you fat reports every day for fat returns. They won't get any place, but you'll be able to spend your money and convince yourself you're doing something.'

She looked me over thoughtfully, as though I were a new coat that might suit her.

'That wasn't very nice.'

The fact that she was right didn't make me feel any better. I was sour on the whole deal.

'I don't feel very nice,' I snarled. 'It's past two in the morning. You weren't very nice to Harrigan, either. He's dumb, sure, but he's straight, and he's only playing this the way he's been told. So you put him over a slow fire. You treat Hillier as though he's dirt. Now it's my turn. I get the bank balance. What's next, or do I have to guess?'

I looked her up and down leeringly. Twin spots of dull red appeared on the high cheek-bones. Every word was now a barb.

'Before I have you thrown out, Mr. Preston, would you mind telling me just why you should speak to me in this way?'

'All right.' I set my empty glass down. 'I don't buy this brave little woman routine. You don't cut any ice with me at all. Suppose your husband was murdered? If you'd been home maybe it wouldn't have happened. If it wasn't murder, it was suicide. And when the brave little woman gets home at one-thirty in the a.m., I could dream up a reason or two why a man should want to blow out his brains. You see, Marcia, I don't believe you want to face up to that fact. You couldn't bear it to be suicide, because that would make it your fault. It has to be murder so you can sleep nights.'

She folded up then. Flung herself sideways across the arm of the chair and began to cry, deep racking sobs that made her whole body shake. I got up awkwardly, cursing myself for a loud-mouthed fool. I didn't quite know whether I ought to get out and leave her in privacy. I settled for another pull at the bottle. After a minute or so, she quietened down and was feeling around for a handkerchief. I put one in her hand and got a muffled thanks in between sobs. Her cheeks were lined with tears.

'I'm sorry,' I said, 'I guess that was pretty raw.'

She shook her head, but made no reply. After another silence, she walked over to the wall mirror and inspected herself. The eyes were slightly swollen, otherwise she looked fine. That was because she wore no make-up to streak. When she spoke there was no trace of any emotion.

'My husband used to say I should have been a business woman. I never let my personal feelings interfere with business matters. When we agreed to engage you to get this little trollop to leave us alone, it was after extensive enquiries, Mr. Preston. Everywhere we looked, the answer was always 'Get Preston'. So we got you.

The fact that you and I don't have a great opinion of one another doesn't prevent my asking you to reconsider your decision about investigating my husband's death.'

I admired her. Whatever she did, Marcia Van Huizen was a lot of woman. And she had me over a barrel now. I couldn't refuse, after the way I'd just spoken to her.

'I don't believe I'm going to produce any results,' I told her, 'but I'll certainly go into the whole thing very thoroughly. One thing I will guarantee. When I produce my report it will satisfy you, one way or the other.'

'Thank you. Will you be too sensitive this time if I mention money?'

I grinned.

'It's taken care of. Hillier gave me an advance of five hundred over this other business. That's hardly been touched.'

I don't know what it was she started to say then, because Hillier suddenly burst into the room. He was excited and breathing quickly.

'Marcia, Harrigan's just — '

'I'll tell her myself, if you don't mind.'

The tall figure of Harrigan appeared beside Hillier, Dunphy hovered in the background.

'I'm sorry to have to break it to you this way, Mrs. Van Huizen, but the girl who was blackmailing your husband has been found murdered in her apartment. She was shot once, with a heavy calibre revolver. Probably a .45.'

Marcia was pale under the tan.

'Murdered?' She whispered the word so quietly I could hardly catch it.

'I'm afraid so. You realise what this means?'

To give him credit, Harrigan was not taking his opportunity to get back at her for the way she'd spoken to him earlier.

'I don't think I follow you, Mr. Harrigan,' she replied.

'It means that subject to a report from ballistics, which I am convinced will be positive, we shall proceed on the assumption that your husband killed the girl, then came back here and shot himself.'

But Marcia hadn't caught the last part. She fainted, and hit the floor before anyone could grab her.

Hillier rushed across and knelt beside her, cradling her face in his arms.

'Did you have to tell her like that?' he protested. 'Couldn't you at least have waited until morning?'

Harrigan shook his head.

'No, son, I couldn't. She forced me to tell her. I had one hour before she was going to turn the heat on, remember?'

I took him by the arm and led him outside.

'I guess that makes this City business now, huh?' I enquired.

Dunphy snorted. He didn't seem to need a very large vocabulary. Harrigan looked at me suspiciously.

'What difference does it make to you? No skin off your nose either way.'

'That's right, I was just curious. Who's handling it that end? Rourke?'

'No, Randall. But maybe Rourke'll get it in the morning. Randall's on his squad, ain't he?'

'Yes,' I replied. Then, 'Well, if that about ties it up for me here, I'd like to see how those pillows are looking today.'

'I guess so,' Harrigan's voice was tired.

'Means I'll be here the rest of the night now.' To Dunphy he said, 'Go see if you can rustle up some coffee, will you? And something to eat. Anything.'

When Dunphy headed for the back of the house, the tall man turned to me.

'Come in here a minute.'

I followed him into the room next to the library.

'Look, Preston, maybe we got off on the wrong foot. Could be I had kind of a wrong idea about you. No hard feelings?'

For a cop he was practically crawling.

'What's the rest of it?' I countered.

'This new thing, about the girl and all, it sure complicates matters.' He went and sat down in an upright armchair. He looked all in. 'I'll look better in the sheets if it reads that the first I knew of the girl was when the widow got home.'

I tried to be easy on him.

'With me it would be O.K., but I don't think you'll be able to square my desperate accomplice.'

I jerked my head back towards the room we'd just left.

'The cream-puff? You don't think he'd

buy?' When I shook my head, he said wearily, 'Ah, what the hell.'

I left him there and crossed the hall to the front door. There was no sound anywhere. Outside a stiff breeze had set up and I shivered slightly. My clothes weren't exactly intended for the present temperature. On the way out I remembered just in time the sharp turn just at the beginning of the drive. I had plenty to think about on the empty coast road back to town.

3

I was back at the beach, sitting on the same rocks. The water was all around, and coming up fast. I knew I had to get out of there, but my foot was caught. I struggled to get it free, and the water was over me now. My heart was thumping like a steam-hammer and I had to get that foot moving. Then I saw through the green blur of the water Dunphy's bloated face, split in an evil smile. He was pressing down with all his strength on the rock holding my foot. With my free leg I kicked at his face, but the water took all the force out of it and the grinning face just moved lazily out of the way. A steel band around my head was getting tighter, and red started to blur my vision. I started shouting with crazy fear. I woke up with the cold sweat all over my face and soaking into the pillow under my head. The covers were every which way, and I was panting as though there was no

71

air left in the room. I fumbled around for a cigarette and lay there for a minute or two, while the acrid smoke burned at the back of my throat. It was nine-thirty in the morning, five and a half hours since I'd arrived back from the Van Huizen place. The whole of that time I'd spent tossing restlessly on the bed, and the one time it looked like I might get some rest, Dunphy had to try to kill me. I cursed Dunphy.

I paddled to the outer door and reached around for the papers. I'd left word with the night man that I wanted them all, and there was quite a lot of paper to pick up. The suicide of Benedict Van Huizen hadn't exactly been given the silent treatment. There it was, right on the front page, pictures and everything. I read everything very carefully. It was the usual mixture every time. Van Huizen was dead, probably a suicide, time of death was 10.30 p.m., the butler found the body. That was the end of the relevant facts in every sheet, but the thing ran to four columns in the lowest coverage, and to seventeen columns in the good old

Monkton News, the yellowest sheet, on the coast. Any coast. The *News* had covered the whole history of the Van Huizen family, back three generations. I got a mention here and there. I was 'the mysterious private investigator Mark Preston' in the *Record*, 'Man-about-town Mark Q. Preston' in the *Banner*. I was intrigued by the 'Q', which was some sub-editor's invention. There was one thing all the stories shared. A total failure to mention Cheryl Vickers. In the *News* I found her on page 12: 'Brutal Slaying of Redhead Beauty,' followed by eight lines which told me one thing. The girl was three months pregnant. Whether the late Van Huizen was the responsible party or not, there was no fake about Cheryl's condition. The other pages all had her story, too, but none of them connected her death with Van Huizen. Marcia, it seemed, must know quite a lot of people. It could be Harrigan's boss, though. The holder of the office of Monkton County Sheriff was a political appointee, and no politician would want any muck raking around a prominent corpse like Van

Huizen until things had been looked into thoroughly.

I tossed the papers on the bed and rang down for some coffee and food. An hour later I felt I might live. The first thing I had to do was get the record straight with the law. I left the car in the parking space beside the headquarters building, under a notice that said something about parking being available only to police officials. A uniformed sergeant sat at a desk inside the glass doors.

'Morning, O'Toole. Rourke around?'

'No. Gil Randall's still here though. He's like a bear with a sore head. Maybe he'll take a bite at you, huh?'

O'Toole sounded quite cheerful at the prospect.

'Could be. I'll go on up and give him a chance.'

The homicide squad doesn't rate very high on the list of appropriations for the city administration. Three rooms on the third floor, all in need of decoration. I passed the first two doors. The third is half-panelled in frosted glass, and the word 'PRIVATE' is stencilled on it. I knocked and went in. Gil Randall was seated behind Rourke's desk, the telephone looking like a toy in his great paw. He glared at me by way of greeting and went on listening. I parked on a spare chair and lit a cigarette. Randall is six feet two inches tall and draws close to two hundred pounds. He's a picture of the typical dumb cop everybody talks about. The jails are full of people who can tell you how dumb he is.

'Yeah. Yeah. Yeah,' he said. Then he varied it. 'O.K.'

He put the instrument back in its cradle and ran his other hand through his crisp black hair.

'Well?' he sounded tired.

'The Cheryl Vickers' murder,' I announced. 'I've come to make a statement.'

'Oh, no,' he groaned. 'Let me tell you something. I finished here after midnight last night. At two-thirty I was hauled out of bed to go and look at some poor kid with a large bullet hole in her. Since then I have been kinda busy. Just when it looks as though I might creep away to the sack, you show up. I know you figure in this. I coulda pulled you out of bed, but I didn't. I thought you could wait,' he said sadly. 'I knew for sure you wouldn't came in without being sent for. Now you're here.'

'As a citizen of this community,' I placed a hand flat on my chest, 'I know it's my duty to tell the police anything I know which may assist in the apprehension of a felon.'

'Ah nuts. Anyway, what have you got? This deal is open and shut.'

'Is it, Gil?'

'Sure. If I wasn't so tired, I wouldn't tell you this, but it happened the way you read it last night.'

'The way I read it?'

'Sure, Harrigan told us you helped him spell it out.'

That was nice of Harrigan. Last I remembered he was doing his own spelling, and looking pretty satisfied with the results. Of course, it could be that he was using me as an excuse to the County Sheriff. A well-known private john right on the scene when inconvenient evidence presents itself. Alone he could have suppressed it, but with me at his elbow, he had no alternative but to, etcetera. Harrigan was looking out for Harrigan.

'So it was Van Huizen, eh?'

'No doubt of it.' Randall shifted some papers and produced a thin folder. 'Ballistics. No possibility of error. It was the same gun.'

I'd never seriously doubted that it would be.

'You talked with Marcia, the guy's widow?'

'Nah. The doc gave her a sedative. Said she'd had enough for one night. We don't really need her anyway, 'cept to make the file tidy.'

I nodded.

'I still think it's crazy. A guy like Van Huizen. Why, he'd got every reason in the world to go on living.'

Randall leaned forward over the table. He was badly in need of a shave.

'Look, Preston. You just got out of a nice warm bed. I been working. Don't give me a fancy routine about this deal. We like it the way it is. This is kind of a busy job, homicide department in

77

Monkton City. For once we got a tidy arrangement. A girl gets pregnant and puts the shake on the guy responsible. The guy kills her, realises what he's done, blows out his brains. It happens every day.'

'Not to millionaires,' I told him.

'Don't ride me. I've had it.'

I only had to look at him to see that was true.

'Just do one little thing for me and I won't bother you any more.'

I took a billfold from my inside jacket pocket. From it I removed the notepaper Hillier had handed me the morning before.

'This is a note from Van Huizen to Hillier. He's telling him to hire me for the blackmail angle.'

'So?'

'I got this yesterday morning. So why would the guy pull a stunt like this without waiting to see how I made out?'

'I don't know. I'd like to know, but we're using the public's money here. Sure, there are one or two things we don't like. But we haven't got the time or the men to button up every little detail. Anyway, both the principals are dead, don't forget that. Case like this you never do know everything. The only people with the real answers are in the morgue.'

'All right, Gil. This favour I mentioned. Get this note verified. I want to know whether the handwriting really is Van Huizen's. And it's no use asking Hillier, it was he gave it to me.'

He took the folded paper from my hand, opened it and read.

'Plain enough,' he observed. 'What's your angle?'

'Nothing definite. Just that I never saw the guy who employed me until his brains were on display. He never told me he wanted me for this job. Other people are the only ones to do that, up till now.'

'I can see what you're driving at. I don't think there's anything in it. All right,' he said quickly, as I opened my mouth to argue, 'I heard you. Just one favour. I'll get it checked, then if it's O.K., you're happy?'

'And if it isn't,' I rejoined, 'you're gonna have to open a new file, right?

Maybe you won't even get to bed tonight either.'

'Now I'll tell you one. You come back here at three this afternoon to make a formal statement. I'll get this looked over in the meantime.'

'Right. Tell me something about the girl.'

'Haven't you gone yet? O.K. What about her?'

'I mean her background. She have any folks?'

Randall sighed. His banana fingers drummed on the table.

'We don't know yet. You know how it is when a dame gets herself that way. She only moved into the apartment four days ago. Nobody asked her where she came from, only if she could promote the rent. She could. The name is probably a phoney, too. But she can't have come from very far. Van Huizen hadn't been out of the State in six months. We've sent her head and shoulders out on the wire. A dame with those looks won't take a lot of checking. We'll know all about her in a day or two.'

I nodded.

'Sure. Well, I'll see you later.'

'Not me, brother. I'm gonna hit the sack. Rourke or somebody can take your statement.'

I left him and went back to the car. A rookie cop watched suspiciously as I backed out of the official parking space and swung out on to the road. I grinned at him, and by way of answer he wrote my number down as I moved away. At the office Miss Digby gave me a chilly reception, so I had to tell her a little about the night's doings. She made a few notes.

'Better put that stuff on the Van Huizen file,' I told her; 'and change the client's name from Benedict to Marcia.'

Florence Digby was puzzled.

'But according to what you just told me, Mrs. Van Huizen engaged you before she heard about the death of this other poor girl. Surely she won't wish you to continue now?'

'I don't know,' I answered. 'Marcia passed out cold when Harrigan told us about Cheryl. So the last thing she said to me was, I was hired. Leave it that way

81

until she changes it.'

'Very well.'

'Oh, and try to raise Sam Thompson, will you?'

The sun was doing its best to turn me into a pot-roast again, when the extension phone in my office rang.

'Sam? Howsa boy? Fine. Listen, I got something for you — no, wait. No walking around. Just a quiet job sitting at a table.'

He mumbled something about not being too well lately. Sam will take more trouble over avoiding work than anybody else I know.

'I want to find a restaurant of some kind. Any kind, just so the name ends in A-T-E'S. Got it? Could be Kate's or something like that. Go down to the public library and dig out all the directories you can find.'

'Any suggestions where I start?' He didn't relish the idea at all.

I took a deep breath.

'Try San Francisco first. I don't promise anything, but it has to be somewhere in this State, and I kind of like that town as an even money bet.'

He thought about it.

'I might find it in ten minutes or it may take a week. What's the deal?'

'Guarantee a ten, more if it takes longer than this afternoon. Call me around four-thirty and let me know what you got so far.'

'Kay.'

Something that could have been the beginnings of an idea was forming in my mind. I couldn't have said exactly why I was bothering with this anyhow. Maybe I felt that the late Benedict Van Huizen hadn't had a fair bargain for his money at the time he died. One way to salve my conscience would have been to send the money back, but that way didn't appeal to me much.

By way of lunch I went back to Parkside and tried a couple of cans of frosted beer, then did my Rip Van Winkle imitation for the better part of two hours. I was coming out of it slowly when somebody pressed the buzzer on the front door of the apartment. Grumbling softly, I heaved myself up and went to answer it.

She was tall, maybe five-eight, well proportioned to match her height. The dress was a cool pink, with a broad black belt around her waist. She had deep black hair and a scarlet mouth that held a promise of many things. The violet eyes looked at me enquiringly.

'Mr. Mark Preston?'

The voice was cool, too. She hadn't acquired it in Monkton City. This gal was all the way from the East Coast.

'What can I do for you?'

'You could ask me in, for one thing. Or do you always do your business in the hall?'

I stood back. As she walked past me, I caught a trace of some perfume that hadn't come from the five and dime.

'Where I usually do business is at my office, Miss — ?'

I let it hang there, where she'd have no trouble picking it up. She let it dangle. She was inspecting the apartment, the deep eyes flicking restlessly from one spot to another.

'I've already paid a year in advance,' I told her. 'Maybe you'd like the number of the estate office.'

She turned to me then and smiled. I liked it. She had one of those warm, friendly smiles that brought out tiny lights in her eyes.

'All women are naturally curious about what kind of places men live in.'

There was something in her directness that appealed to me. And that wasn't all.

'Let's get on with it, lady. I have to go out in a few minutes.'

By way of reply she sat down gracefully in one of my upright chairs. It had never looked so good. She was staying. I sighed gently and proffered my pack of Old Favourites. Then I had to light it for her.

'You're a private eye, a shamus. That right?' She looked at me coolly.

I was looking at her, too. All over, and it didn't help to keep me cool.

'That's what I claim. What can I do for you?'

'I want you to work for me. I'll pay well. In fact, I'll pay practically anything.'

'What's the rest of it?' I enquired.

'Find out who murdered Benedict Van Huizen.'

She could have fooled me. If she'd said 'go climb Everest', I'd have half-expected it at least. The Van Huizen bit was out of the blue. I studied her carefully. There was no sign of any agitation. Her face remained serene, and the blue smoke rose in a steady straight line from the cigarette gripped between the index and middle fingers of her right hand.

'You go too fast for me. Way I heard it the man committed suicide.'

'No.'

It was final. A decisive, flat negative. She leaned further back against the chair, breasts pushing impatiently against the pink material. If she didn't know what a lot of woman she was, it was time somebody told her. But it wasn't going to be me. Not then.

'You must have some reason for coming to see me like this. What is it?' I asked.

'I just told you. I want you to find out — '

I interrupted quickly.

'Yeah, yeah, I got all that. I meant you had to have some reason for saying what you did just now. Why should this be murder?'

'It's murder all right.'

'The police think different. Have you been to them?'

She moved her head slowly from side to side.

'That wouldn't do anybody any good. Just give the smear sheets some free copy. I was his mistress.'

It was such an old-fashioned word for a new-fashioned girl to use. A little blunt, too, for most people. The majority of women would have hedged around that part for hours. I returned her level gaze and said softly,

'He was a lucky guy.'

'We've been together a couple of years now. Just like old married people.'

If there was any bitterness in her voice, I couldn't trace it.

'I'm not going to tell you it was a great romance. It was an arrangement, and we kept it that way. Ben was always good to me, and very generous. In his own way he was very fond of me. I was fond of him, too. That's why I'm here.'

Not for the first time I found myself envying a guy with that much money. A wife who looked like Marcia, and he could still dream up an 'arrangement' with a whole woman like this. Enough of a woman to want to spend his money catching his killer, if there was one.

'I think you're on the level,' I said.

Her eyes said she was grateful for that.

'Before we go any further, how about a name?'

She hesitated.

'Rona Parsons,' she said finally.

'Uh-huh.'

Quickly I leaned across and snatched up the little black purse she'd been carrying. Her hand started to move towards it, but much too late. I rifled through the pink inside. Compact, keys, a small roll of bills, comb. Then there was an envelope. It was addressed to Mrs. Rona Parsons, Apartment B, Hove Building, W. 70th S.F. Behind the envelope my fingers curled round something hard. I took out a small pearl-handled .22 calibre revolver. It was a beautiful piece of work and weighed scarcely anything. I broke it out, and noted the six neat little cartridges resting in their chambers.

'Satisfied?'

She sat quite still looking up at me.

'Sorry about that,' I said, 'you'd be surprised the phoney names I get sometimes.'

She held out her hand for the purse. I passed it back, slipping the gun into my other hand.

'What's the idea of the hardware?'

She shrugged.

'Girl has to look after herself in this world.'

'No other reason?'

'No.'

'Let's talk about Mr. Parsons. How'd he like the idea of Van Huizen and you being so friendly?'

She said in a tired voice,

'I haven't seen him for eleven years. He walked out one night to get some cigarettes and he didn't come back. It was the happiest night of my life.'

'Not so good, huh?'

'Not good at all. Still that's a long time

ago. Why the cross-examination? What do you care?'

I grinned. She was an easy girl to grin at.

'I wanted to hear you tell it. I wanted to watch you while you talked. I'm trying to decide whether I can trust you.'

'Oh.'

There'd been scarcely any trace of emotion in anything she said or did. Rona Parsons was one of the cool ones. She'd been there, and it wasn't nice. Now she took it slow and easy. I thought I'd tell her.

'Rona, this isn't a very nice thing to hear, but I figure you for the close-mouthed variety. There's more to Van Huizen's suicide than just his own death.'

She was listening all right, every line of her superb body tuned to what I was saying.

'It seems there was a girl. Another girl.'

The look on her face was disbelief.

'That's a lie.'

I held up a hand.

'Now hold on. There's more. This girl was pregnant. She was blackmailing Van

Huizen over it. He killed her here in town, then drove home and blew his own brains out.'

'No, no, I don't believe it. Not a word.'

She was shaken now, visibly less calm than before. I said, as gently as I could,

'It was the same gun, Rona. The scientific lab. doesn't make mistakes about things like that. The bullets match exactly.'

She took it well.

'You were there, weren't you? Last night. I saw your name in the paper.'

I nodded.

'Where was she when he died?'

'She?'

'Marcia. The garbage man's lay. Where was she?'

'We're not going to get any place calling names. What did you mean by that crack, lady?'

'Marcia?' She smiled. It wasn't nice. 'Why d'you think Ben had me? He needed some kind of a home, that's why. I was faithful to him. I didn't love him or any of that stuff, but I was there when he wanted me. He kept me, and I was faithful to him. Does that surprise you?'

'No. With you it doesn't. I'd almost expect it.' It was the truth.

'Thanks. It wasn't like that with Marcia. With her it is anybody any time. Was she there? Could she have killed him?'

I was busy digesting this new stuff about Marcia Van Huizen. Certainly I'd seen her looking more than friendly with Ed Newman the night before. Hillier, too, had seemed quite at home around the house. But, of course, he would. He was the guy's personal assistant, wasn't he? Out loud I said,

'You're off the beam, Rona. She wasn't even home till hours after it happened. I was there when she arrived. She was all cut up over this.'

'I'll bet.' Rona got up suddenly and walked to the window. She stood looking out for a while. Neither of us spoke. Then, 'Do you think you could believe me a little longer if I told you something, Preston?'

'Try me,' I suggested.

'Well, here it is. Benedict Van Huizen

was a moral man.' She turned away from the view and faced me. 'The kind of man little boys are taught to be when they grow up. Only they never are. He was ashamed of what he called his weakness in keeping me. But he had no choice. Marcia, his dear wife, is worse than any alley cat. He had to have somebody, and I was lucky. Yes, lucky. He was a good man, a fine man, and married to a lousy chippie. How do you like that?'

'There's more, isn't there?'

'Plenty. I'll take my oath he wasn't responsible for that girl's condition, the one who got killed. It was a frame. The whole thing is a frame. The man was murdered. Won't you please help me find out who did it? Please?'

There was no getting over her sincerity, no ignoring her conviction. It wasn't going to be easy to fob her off.

'But what can I do? The police are satisfied. They've practically closed their files already. I'm just one man. I have a licence, but no badge. Even if you were right, I wouldn't know where to start.'

I'd been too gentle trying to talk round

it that way. I should have been plain rough, and showed her the door. Now she could see I was hesitating she dived in.

'I'll tell you where you could start. With Doctor Cosmo Peterson.'

'Peterson? Who's he?' I thought the name rang a faint bell.

'He's a big medical man. Specialises in cardiac problems.'

Now I'd got it. Peterson was the man who had represented this country on the team that had recently returned from studying the medical requirements in some of the overcrowded territories in the Pacific. I'd read some stuff about him in one of the glossy mags not long before. Rona wasn't exaggerating when she said he was a big medical man. He was the biggest.

'So he's a heart man. Where does that get us?'

She was composed again now. I didn't know it then, but the slight relaxation of Rona's calm which I'd experienced over the past few minutes was practically a full-scale explosion of temper for her. It was as near as she ever got to blowing a fuse. Well, almost.

'Ben knows — knew Petersen. Went to see him only last week. The doctor is giving a four-week period of his services to the Navy at the moment.'

'Where?'

'San Diego. Ben went over there and had dinner with him last — let me see — Wednesday. Yes, it was Wednesday,' she confirmed.

'So? He knew him, didn't he? Why shouldn't he go see the man?'

She opened her eyes wide. The violet pupils were a knockout.

'No reason at all. But for a couple of days after that Ben was fretful, almost moody for him. He was a quiet, kind man. Not given to bad temper or moods. It's my guess something happened between him and Petersen, something that upset him.'

'And he couldn't talk about it?'

She shook her head.

'Uh, uh. Practically bit my head off when I suggested it.'

As gently as possible I said,

'That just could have been because you

were wrong, huh?'

'It could.'

She walked across and picked up her purse. Diving her fingers inside she pulled out a piece of paper and handed it to me. It was coarse in texture, had a picture of Benjamin Franklin on it, together with a lot of fancy penmanship. In the part where it counts it read, '500 Dollars'. Rona said,

'I want you to find out whether I'm wrong or not. There's plenty more where that came from, and I'm not afraid to spend it.'

I thought she was wrong. I thought she was letting her emotion over Van Huizen's death get the better of her common sense. I also thought she'd handed me a five-hundred-dollar retainer and if I didn't take it, she'd soon find someone who would.

'I think you're mistaken over this. I don't know enough about the late Mr. Van Huizen to say whether he had any motive for suicide or not. What I do know is that police investigators have put his death down as suicide, and they are people who are trained to look. However,' I held up a hand as she seemed about to interrupt, ' . . . for five hundred dollars it becomes my business. I'll look around a little bit on my own account.'

She was grateful. The red lips parted in one of those smiles again. It would be nice to have Rona Parsons around often, together with the smile and the rest of her. Unfortunately I was pushed for time at that moment.

'If you've nothing else to tell me, I've an appointment at police headquarters at three.'

'One thing. You'll find Dr. Petersen at the Mowbray Hotel in San Diego. I don't think he'll be free to see anybody until evening, according to what Ben said.'

'Okay, thanks.'

She gathered her stuff together and walked to the door.

'When shall I hear from you?'

'Can't be sure. I'll get in touch with you tomorrow some time to let you know what's happening. But remember, I'm not promising anything.'

'I'll remember.'

I opened the door for her. She held out her hand. I'd forgotten the toy gun in my jacket pocket.

'Thank you.' She slipped it back inside her purse. 'You can reach me at the address on the envelope you saw.'

'Fine.' I grinned at her. It was easy to do. 'How about the phone?'

'I'm in the book.' She was holding her hand out again. I took it and we shook briefly. For two cents I'd have pulled her to me, and she must have sensed it. 'I'll look forward to seeing you again, when you've something to tell me.' Then she was gone.

I watched her out of sight then closed the door regretfully. Whatever else I was going to find out about Van Huizen, nobody was going to persuade me to doubt his taste in women. Both his wife and his girl friend were something extra special, and both of them wanted to spend their own money saving his good name. Then there was Cheryl who claimed to have been carrying his child. She was a beauty, too, before somebody blew a large black hole in her breast.

Come to think of it, Marcia Van Huizen hired me before she heard about Cheryl's murder. Maybe that wiped the slate as far as she was concerned. That was one angle I'd have to check early. I was working for Rona Parsons already, but there's no law to say I can't draw two pay-cheques for carrying out the same investigation.

I had plenty to think about on my way to headquarters.

4

The room hadn't changed. The same scarred tables, battered once-grey file cabinets, metal desk lamp. The face across the desk was different.

' 'Lo, Schultzie, I'm expected.'

Schultz grunted and sorted through some papers. He was one of Rourke's new men. Ex-patrolman, with high markings at his graduation. Rourke had waited the regulation four months that every rookie cop has to spend pounding the sidewalk. Then he rushed through a requisition to have Schultz assigned to him, before some other branch of the department could get around to it. He thought very highly of his protege's ability, and Rourke is known as a man with an eye for promising material. Like most new boys, Schultz was a guy with both eyes firmly glued to the regulations. I knew he was horrified at times, the way Rourke and Randall and the other more experienced men would chew the fat with every crook in town. Shady characters included people with private licences in Schultz's book, and that meant me.

'You're late,' he greeted, and jerked a thumb at the aged wall clock. It stood at five minutes after three.

'Tut, tut,' I said gently. 'And no excuse either. You ought to be able to think up some charge for that, Schultzie.'

His smooth young face darkened.

'Don't come in here riding me, Preston. I bounce better guys than you off the wall every morning.'

'My, such strength of character.'

I wasn't meaning to needle him too much. He'd have to learn to keep his temper if he was going to make the detective squad as a permanent career. He was learning at that. Now he took a deep breath, swallowed mightily and said, in a choked voice,

'All right, peeper. Let's have a statement from you about last night. And keep out the humour.'

I kept out the humour. A police stenographer came in to take it down.

When I got a look at her, I knew I wasn't going to have any trouble concentrating on what I was saying. It was to be hoped that she made up in efficiency what she lacked in other directions. The whole thing took about thirty minutes. When she'd gone I asked,

'Rourke around?'

Schultz shook his head. He was much more human now he was working to the rules, taking a statement from a witness and stuff.

'No. I expected him when you showed up. He ought to be here any minute.' Then he changed the subject, 'Say, that guy Hillier, did he play ball some time? I don't mean the big game, but good college ball?'

'We didn't get around to ball games,' I told him. 'Could be though. Why do you ask?'

'I used to follow it a little. I remember his face from somewhere. Nice guy, huh?'

'Sure.'

We sat around, smoking and waiting while the stenographer typed up my statement. Finally the door opened. It was Rourke. Schultz vacated the chair in a hurry. Rourke spoke to him ignoring me.

'Well, did he confess?'

'Confess?' Bewilderment spread plain over the young cop's face.

'Sure. You've had him in here over half an hour. He shoulda confessed to something.'

Schultz looked at me in painful embarrassment. I winked at him. He stammered.

'I ought to get along to fingerprints, chief. That waterfront thing.'

He scuttled out of the door. Rourke beamed broadly.

'Did he use the rubber hose on you, Mark?'

'He'll be O.K., John. Been practically civil most of the time.'

'Good stuff, that boy. Once we get rid of this crime crusader complex of his, he'll pull some weight around here.'

'I hope he makes it,' I replied.

The stenographer came in with a neat pile of typescript which she placed in front of the lieutenant. He picked it up and started to read. I knew better than to interrupt. It took him a long time, then when he was done, he tilted back his head and stared at the grimy ceiling for a full minute.

'Yeah, I guess so. I guess it fits all right. Here.'

He tossed the top sheets over to me and I read quickly. It was exactly the way I'd told it.

'You wanta sign that?'

I nodded, and picked up a pen from the table. Then he handed over the rest of the paper.

'And the carbons. Three copies, Mark.'

I signed everything in sight and handed it all back to him. He wrinkled his forehead in puzzlement.

'Kind of a new spot for you, huh?'

'How d'ya mean, John?'

'I mean not being under suspicion of anything. A real innocent bystander. Must be quite a milestone in your life.'

'How's for an innocent milestone to ask a question or so?'

He got wary.

'What about?'

I tapped an Old Favourite against my thumbnail and snapped my pocket lighter.

'About how slow the Press are. Why haven't they cottoned on to this murder and suicide bit? I mean Cheryl Vickers. Don't tell me some bad policeman is holding up the story.'

Rourke toyed with a flat wooden ruler.

'My business is with the law, not the newspapers. The Vickers girl gets murdered, that's my headache. I'm supposed to find out who did it and if possible why. Well, after some talk with the boys from the County Sheriff's Office, I'm satisfied I have the answer to both those questions. I can put the lid on the case, and this — ' he tapped at my statement ' — is just about the last nail to be hammered in.'

'So why not tell the scribes?' I insisted.

'Dammit to hell, Preston, you know my position.' He slapped the ruler down on the table. The leaves of paper lifted in the sudden breeze. 'I'm a copper, not a blasted politician. And the politicians run this town, including this department. Don't you forget it.'

'You mean the story stays on the table until you get the release from higher up.'

He nodded. Rourke is an honest man, and whenever he finds the law being used as a political convenience, his blood boils. With only eight years to run for his pension, he was reaching a stage where he had to toe the line, or face a hungry old age. He didn't like the position too well. Now he said in a low voice,

'It isn't here so much. Something over at the County end. Seems to me they've asked our people to soft pedal on this one awhile. Lord knows why. The whole thing is open and shut.'

'That's what Harrigan said,' I told him.

'He did? Harrigan's not such a bad feller when you know him. Smart, too. He's got his orders over this, same as me.'

'I don't see what anybody has to gain,' I remarked. 'You can't hush up a murder indefinitely. Somebody'll start asking questions.'

'I know,' said Rourke bitterly. 'And do you know what's gonna happen when they do? Everybody in town is going to ask what kind of a police department this is. And if they ask loud enough, somebody will feel a cold breeze around here. And you get no prize for guessing who that lucky guy will be.'

'Still,' I kept at him, 'it's strange that City Hall is willing to go along with this just to oblige the County Administration.'

He snorted.

'Strange? They're all the same, feller. All those apple-polishing vultures. They're all the same. 'Close down one murder, Joe? Sure, Joe. Say, Joe, you won't forget about that building contract for the new hospital? Swell, Joe, leave it to me'.'

I couldn't argue with him. He was right, clear down the line. Then he said,

'Anyway, what's the use in talking about it?' He switched subjects abruptly. 'Say, what was this thing over the note Van Huizen wrote to Hillier about hiring you?'

'Nothing special. Like I told Gil Randall this morning, it's just that I never saw the guy until he was dead. It made me curious about a few things. Like whether he really wrote that note, for example.'

He nodded, as though thinking of something else.

'It's been checked and double-checked by real experts. I even took it to a guy outside the Department as a saving bet. The note is genuine, clear McCoy from start to finish.'

He reached inside his jacket and pulled out a folded sheet of paper which I recognised as the one Hillier had given me. I took it from him and tucked it in a pocket.

'Well, thanks anyway, John.'

I walked over to the door, then with it half open, turned as if I'd just remembered something.

'Say, what do you hear about George Porter these days?'

Rourke got red around the neck. Nothing a policeman hates worse than being reminded of a crooked ex-colleague.

'That crumb. Why?'

'Just wondered. Haven't seen him around for a while. Thought he might have quit town or something.'

He breathed heavily.

'I'd pay his fare myself if I thought he'd

stay away. No, last I heard he was marking cues or something at Anselmo's.'

'Uh-huh,' I wasn't especially interested. 'Well, I'll see you, Tim.'

He growled something that may have been goodbye.

Anselmo's is a billiards joint down near the harbour. In between a friendly game of pushing the ivory balls around, you could find guys willing to help you heist a bank, distribute reefers, or merely assist in a filling-station stick-up if times were hard. A steep flight of stone steps that led up from the street was the only way in or out. Nobody paid any attention to me. Although it was not yet five in the afternoon, the place was in semi-darkness with brilliant triangles of light over the green tables. A few characters made a pretence of playing. I stood and watched one guy, a loose-limbed, lanky Mexican. In his hands the slender cue was like a violin. The balls trickled this way and that, spinning and cavorting any way he chose. I made a note not to play this guy for money.

I pushed through a door at the side. It

was a square, plain room with a desk in one corner. A fat Italian sat in a leather-padded chair. He had on a violet waistcoat, and a shirt in red and yellow-striped silk. His black greasy hair was pushed carefully into waves and the black moustache was the kind the bandits always have in those South American movies. He was talking in rapid Italian to a swarthy kid who stood by the desk, listening intently.

'Hi, Bonnie,' I said cheerfully.

'Hey, Preston.' The fat face wreathed into a thousand creases, and he lumbered up from the chair to come and shake hands. 'How you bin, huh? Long time you don't come to see old Anselmo, huh?' He was pummelling and pushing at me with excitement.

'I been kinda tied up, Bonnie.'

'It'sa no matter. Finally you get here.'

He led me back to where he'd been sitting, then seeing the kid he stopped smiling and said,

'Alberto, you go now. Tell your mama what I say, huh?'

The kid nodded quickly and made for

the door like a scared rabbit. Anselmo shrugged.

'My nephew. Got a fine education. Some day maybe he should get to be a doctor or something. So what does he do? Hangs around with a bunch of no-account punks who ain't gonna mean nothin' but plenty trouble.'

Always the same tale. I never knew a crook who didn't want the kids in his family to take up some legitimate way of making a living. I took a seat and we talked about this and that for a while. I always had a soft spot for Bonnie Anselmo since the time he tipped me off about three guys who were going on a hunting expedition. In place of the usual sporting rifles, they had sawn-off shotguns. I was to be the grouse. When we'd chattered through enough of the polite formalities I said,

'Hear you gave George Porter a job outside. That right?'

He shrugged his great shoulders. 'Sure. I got nothin' against this man. He needa job. I give.'

'I didn't see him when I came through.

What time does he start?'

'Wassa matter, Mark? You want this guy very bad?'

I shook my head.

'Nothing like that. He ain't in any trouble that I know of. But he could maybe help me with a little something I'm working on.'

Bonnie stuck his two fat hands against his knees.

'I tell you, Mark. This Porter, he's a big disappointment to Anselmo. Two week ago he come here. He need work, need food. I give him, why not? Then he come and go as he please. Sometimes drunk, sometimes very drunk. Then he don't come at all no more.'

'When was he here last?'

He thought about it. Any point further back in time than yesterday always means a great mental struggle to Anselmo. Suddenly his brow cleared.

'I got. Sat'day. Friday he come, Sat'day he'sa no show. Sure. It was Sat'day.'

'What makes you so sure of the day, Bonnie?'

'Sat'day big business for Anselmo,

always. This week, no Porter. One my cousins have to come help me out. Yeah,' he nodded, 'Sat'day.'

There was nothing more to learn from him. As soon as I could, I left and made my way slowly down the grey stone steps. I walked as far as the corner. There was a news-stand with a blind man sitting patiently beside it. This was Blind Ike, one of the most reliable sources of information in the whole town.

'How goes it, Ike?'

The alert face twisted at once towards the sound of my voice.

'Well, well, Mr. Preston of the private eye Prestons. I ain't seen you lately.'

It's a standing gag of Ike's. I replied.

'That's about right. How're things, Ike?'

'Well, you know it's a soft touch for a guy like me. Everybody always rushing around to do me favours. I got it nice.'

I looked at the threadbare suit.

'You always did beat the table, Ike.'

Ike is a guy who likes to talk. He sits at that news-stand from first light until midnight or worse, every day of his life.

It's his office and drawing-room, all in one. Everybody stops off and gabs it up with Ike whenever they have the time. That's how he picks up all his information. He doesn't mind telling you anything that seems harmless enough to repeat. The only qualification is ten minutes of chewing the fat before you get to the point. I strung along until he led me into my routine.

'Say, what brings you into a high-class neighbourhood like this, anyway?'

'I just went up to the Italian's. Wanted a word with George Porter.'

An expression of extreme distaste rooted on the blind man's features. You had to say one thing for Porter. He sure produced the same reaction in everybody.

'You keep bad company, Preston. Anyhow, Porter didn't come to work today. Last I heard, he's moved up in the world.'

'I'll buy. What does that mean, in English?'

'Porter's been laying up in a trap on Harbour Street these many months. Suddenly he packs his roll and moves out.

114

I hear he told one of the other guys he was finished with this kind of life.'

Could be something there. It's a long journey from a rat-hole in Harbour Street to the restaurant of the Club Rendezvous.

'Maybe he reformed or something,' I suggested.

'Be your age. The only way for Porter is down. No.' Ike was serious, 'the way it looks to me, this guy Porter found an in to some nice quick green stuff.'

'Good,' I returned cheerfully. 'Maybe he'll have enough to drink himself to death.'

'Amen. I will be the last to contribute,' was his laconic comment.

'Any idea where I look for him?'

We were interrupted then by a passer-by. He walked up to the stand, riffled through the papers, took one, threw a coin into the metal box. Ike sighed.

'Some of 'em are like that. Can't spare even a minute for a friendly word.'

For a moment or two neither of us spoke. I was beginning to fear that the blind newsman had forgotten my question.

'Course, I ain't a big famous detective or anything like that. I mean I only got my smeller to work with, but I figure like this. When a guy comes down in the world, he figures on going back up some day. Not just any old up, but up the same slide he came down.' He paused, as if expecting a question.

'And?'

'And if it was Porter, and he suddenly found an oil well or something, I would guess he'd head straight back to his old apartment in the Hacienda.'

Before he'd finished talking, I was sure he was right. It must have rankled with Porter, having to leave his swank-lay-out at the Hacienda, a lay-out paid for by extortion and hush money. It would be quite natural for him to go back there if he could ever afford it.

'Ike,' I said solemnly, 'it's a great relief to me you're in the newspaper business. If you ever decide to become a gumshoe, I should be around Harbour Street in no time.'

He grinned.

'Any time. If you're going to have any hard words with the guy, give him one for me, will you?'

'Deal.' I clapped him on the shoulder, tucking a five-spot into his lapel pocket. 'So long, Ike.'

'Be seein' ya.'

The offices of the *Monkton City Globe* are situated between Seventh and Fairfax in the business section. I went inside and stuck my head through a square hole in the partition that divided the editing staff from the corridor.

'Hi Shad.'

Shad Steiner looked sideways up at me, his aged face lined with a thousand forgotten suspicions.

'Well, well, the poor man's Sam Spade. What's new?'

'How's to spend a while in the morgue?'

He screwed up his forehead but there was no room for any more wrinkles.

'What's the story?'

I told him a story. It was a sad little yarn about Hilda Brooks who'd last been

117

seen three or four years ago in Monkton, and whose old folks up in Oregon were trying to trace her. Anything on the files might give me a lead, especially anything under the 'Police' classification because; it was to be confessed, poor Hilda had strayed from the path. Frequently. When I was through Shad muttered,

'I saw Norma Shearer in that one nearly thirty years ago. Sue.'

A scrubbed kid of about seventeen bounced up from nowhere.

'Yes, Mr. Steiner.'

Her voice was like the rest of her. Eager.

'This gentleman,' he stuck a thick thumb towards me, 'Wants to look at some old files. Go down and give him a hand, huh?'

'You bet.'

She bounced away towards the door, and a few seconds later appeared at the end of a passage waving me on. I followed her down two flights of stone steps. She chattered the whole time and I found she was a subject for selective listening. You know the trick. All you do is listen to every twentieth word and you can keep in touch. She led me to a row of aged green file cupboards.

'This is the Police Section,' she announced. 'Of course it's sub-divided.'

She went on to tell me about the system. This time I listened.

'So if I pull out this drawer here,' I pointed, 'I find criminal matters dating three years back?'

'And up to six years ago in that particular drawer. Further back you'll need to — '

'Well, thanks, honey,' I said. 'This'll be enough to start on.'

I was probably crazy anyway, but things I'd heard up to now led me to thinking a certain way. I opened the first folder. It's amazing how many different kinds of trouble people can find to get into. Some of it was very interesting. Too interesting. I made a rule. Names and photographs only. That way I found myself moving along a lot faster. Even so, I was near the end of the eighth folder and closer to four years back than three when I found it.

FOIL EXTORTION RACKET

'Police moved quickly today to smash attempted extortion by twenty-five year old Dean Hillier and beautiful Ivy Hart.'

★   ★   ★

I read it all very carefully. A 'Prominent business man' as the papers insisted, had got tangled up with one Ivy Hart. Her husband had suddenly appeared and threatened to expose the man unless he paid up. It's a very old routine, but one which usually pays off. Not this time. The sucker had more guts than usual and the police grabbed the 'husband' on a charge of extortion. At the bottom was a flash picture of Dean Hillier arriving at police headquarters. The accompanying officer was none other than George Melvin Porter. There was no picture of Ivy Hart, who was due to be picked up at any minute, according to the report. I turned back to the next edition and got a rehashed version of the same tale. After that there were only odd references to the case until three weeks later when it was announced that the victim had changed his mind about pressing charges and Hillier had been released. They never did catch up with Ivy.

I made a careful note of the dates involved and closed up the files. Bouncing Sue had long since lost all interest in me and disappeared. It was a mild relief. I didn't want anybody with Shad Steiner's high savvy content latching on to what I'd found out.

★   ★   ★

When I got to the office Miss Digby was just tidying up her desk, ready to leave. She looked at me severely.

'Anything break, Miss Digby?'

'Unless you count Sam Thompson, no.'

Since I packed Sam off to the City Library I'd been too busy to think much about him.

'What's the word with Sam?'

'I suggest he could answer that better than I.'

She inclined her head towards my office.

'How long's he been here?'

'Almost an hour. If there's nothing further for me tonight — ?'

'Sure, sure, go ahead. I'll see you tomorrow some time.'

I went on in. Sam was prostrate in my softest chair. He's short, tubby and balding. A craggy face surrounding two heavy-lidded eyes might give an impression of stupidity, but you'd be wrong. Sam is not stupid at all, just lazy, and with nearly forty years' practice.

'Sorry about this, Sam. I didn't realise you'd call in with the stuff.'

He wiggled a finger by way of answer. Then he held up a piece of paper. I took it and smoothed it out. In heavy square capitals it read: —

KATE'S PLACE
THE SENATE BAR AND GRILL
NATE'S
TINPLATE'S GRILL
HECATE'S HAMBURGER GRILL

'This is the full run-down, huh?'

'That's all, Preston. If you'll pay me now, I'll blow.'

'Hold on a minute.'

I ran down them again.

'Tell me what you know about these places, huh, Sam?'

With a deep sigh he heaved himself into what passes for an upright position with him.

'They're all harmless, except maybe Nate's.'

'What's with Nate's?'

'You could most likely get the H there if you wanted. It's a drug store used by the high school crowd.'

'You're cute,' I told him. 'Let's have the rest of your repertoire.'

'I'll start with Kate's Place. Seems there are three such.'

He took me on a roving tour of the hash houses on the list. Sam has a gift of description. Economical with words, but they're the right words. It was a description of these places that would have done credit to a police file. It was lucky for me that Sam was a San

Francisco man himself. He was saving me a lot of shoe leather. The third of the Kate series sounded worthy of a second look. I made a note in my mind, but didn't interrupt him. The Senate Bar and Grill, too, could have been what I was looking for.

'You remember a fighter just before Pearl Harbour? Terence O'Keefe?' he asked.

'O'Keefe? No, I don't think I'm with it.'

'Sure you are,' he snorted. 'Guy got roughed up some in an auto accident. They had to operate on his skull, put one of those silver plates in his head.'

It's a sore point with Sam when he mixes with people who weren't all grown up before the Second World War. He figures it dates him alongside prehistoric man. I pretended to puzzle over it.

'Something does buzz a little,' I said. 'Just can't place it exactly.'

'Keep trying. After that they billed him as Tinplate Terence. He didn't last, because guys were afraid to hit him in the head in case he croaked.'

'Oh, yeah. It does seem familiar now,' I conceded.

'There, you see. Anyhow, instead of buying himself a bar, like so many of those guys, he put his shirt on the hash business. He figured that fighters do more eating than boozing, and he might as well get behind the cash register. That's Tinplate's Grill, now. All the fighters and managers use the place as a kind of headquarters.'

He told me some more about it. Then he moved on to the last one.

'Hecate's is a place for screwballs. This Hecate is a dame, one of the artistic ones. The joint is dolled out like a studio and the counter is shaped like a painter's pallette. She draws the poets and the long-hairs, also a few queers of one kind and another. No place to take a hairy chest or an appetite.'

I pumped in a few questions about Hecate's. Sam Thompson had earned his money, in spades. I pushed some bills across the desk. He picked them up, started to shove them in his pocket, then drew his hand back and looked at the money.

'Hey, this is too much. There's twenty bucks here,' he protested.

'So? It's genuine. You can bet I'll charge it up to a client.'

He nodded doubtfully, and pushed the money deep into his pants' pocket.

'Well, if you're sure it's O.K. Thanks.'

When he'd gone I picked up the telephone. I had some calls to make and I was extra polite to the little lady operator who was going to have to do most of the work at the end of this long hot day. First I got through to the third Kate's Place.

'Is this Kate's?'

A woman's voice said: 'Kate speaking.'

'I want to talk with Cheryl. Is she there?'

'Cheryl?' She sounded puzzled. 'Cheryl who?'

'Her married name is Vickers, but I don't know whether she might be using her single name now. And I don't know what that is.'

She thought that over. I could guess what she was making of it.

'Well, I'm sorry, but we don't have a Cheryl anything here.'

'Look,' I made myself sound desperate, 'look, this is a matter of real importance. If she comes in, or anybody asks after her, will you take a note of my name and number?'

'But I don't see what use — '

'Please.'

'Well, it's a waste of time, I can assure you, but if it'll make you feel any better.'

I told her my name and gave her the office telephone number. She took a little more interest, it seemed to me, when I mentioned Monkton City, but that could have been merely because it ruled me out as a gag-man. Jokers do not call semi-long-distance. I thanked her too many times and replaced the receiver. Then I picked it up and went into my act again for the benefit of a guy with a high-pitched voice who claimed to be the manager of the Senate Bar and Grill. Wearily I plodded my way down the list. The only bit of excitement was when I talked to Nate. Yes, he knew a Cheryl and yes, he'd give her my message. He'd also give it to her parents and the San Francisco Police Department, just to be on the safe side. Cheryl was fifteen years old, and he'd heard about guys like me before. Otherwise it was the same routine every time. When I was through, I wrote out some notes for Florence Digby. There was an outside chance that one of the calls might produce something, and Florence would have been in the dark unless I left her some instructions on what to do. One more thing to do before I closed the office. I picked up the phone and dialled a number.

'Monkton City Airport.'

'Any chance of a local round trip tonight? San Diego?'

'Just one moment, please.'

There was some plug pushing, and a honeyed voice took over.

'I have your enquiry, sir. There is one flight leaving for San Diego at seven-ten this evening. After that it would mean the eleven o'clock I'm afraid.'

I could see this one, a smooth blonde in one of those lightweight chocolate uniforms, with the little cap pushed slightly wider of centre than the regulations said. The voice was cool.

'The seven-ten would be fine. Could I get back tonight?'

'Let me see.'

I could hear her turning the pages of the schedule. She was taking as much trouble over my jaunt as though it was a through flight to Tokyo. I liked that. Truth was, I could have got there by car in a little over two hours, but that would mean two hours back as well, and all that driving in one evening held no particular appeal. Finally she came back.

'There is just one chance. The routine night flight from San Diego at ten-thirty has one unconfirmed reservation at present. Of course, I couldn't guarantee it won't be taken up before departure time.'

'I'll take a chance, honey. The name is Preston, Mark Preston.'

We chinwagged about addresses and passage money and stuff and I was all set. Even if it turned out I wasn't able to grab the late plane back, it wouldn't matter too much. I could sleep just as well in San Diego as in Monkton City, and catch a trip back in the morning. According to my watch it was now six-twenty, which meant I didn't have a lot of time to waste. I locked up the office and headed for Parkside.

My clothes were sticking to me with the heat. It was a relief to peel them off and get cleaned up. I was wandering around the same way I came into the world, except I was holding a glass, when the telephone jangled.

'Yeah?'

'Is that you, Preston?' It was Hillier's voice.

'Uh huh. What's up?'

'Listen. I've got to see you. It's important.' He sounded excited.

'You'll have to snap it up. I'm catching a plane pretty soon. Can you come round right away?'

'I'm at the house. It'll take me an hour to get to you.' He seemed to be talking in a sibilant whisper, as though afraid of being overheard.

'I'll be gone before then. Look, with any luck, I'll be back around midnight. Why not make it then?'

'That's the earliest you can do?'

'I guess it is.'

'All right, I'll come there then.'

'I'll leave a key with the night man and tell him you're coming.'

'Thanks. See you later then.'

I cursed the plane trip softly. There was so much around this thing I didn't know, whatever Hillier told me was likely to be news. Now that I knew more about the guy, I was especially interested in a little talk with him. Still it was a delay of only a few hours at the most. It would keep.

5

The airport at Monkton City is not as big as Idlewild. It's really not much more than a huddle of buildings standing at the end of one leg of a huge concrete cross. There were six or seven liners, none of them overbig, standing patiently while hordes of busy people swarmed round them. I parked outside the control tower — always do if I'm taking a trip. The public parking space provided is home from home for the guys who drive off in cars belonging to other people. I just leave mine unattended and in plain view outside the control building. Anybody interested enough to look would naturally assume the heap belonged to one of the guys working inside who may be coming off duty any minute.

I walked into the passengers' hall. There seemed to be quite a few people around, either waiting for the next flight in or out, or else seeing somebody off on a trip. The offices led off to one side. I leaned through a small hole in the wall and looked into an empty cubicle. Then I pushed the buzzer.

'Can I help you, sir?'

It was the honeyed voice of the girl who'd made the reservation for me. I turned my head with an anticipating smile. She was tubby with mousy fair hair and unattractive ornamental spectacles. These were wing-shaped at the corners, and done in some red plastic stuff. Her eyes were lustreless, and there was no life in the pale, flabby skin. On balance she looked like a surprised female Mephistopheles. I swallowed, but desperately hung on to the grin.

'Why, yes, thank you. The name is Preston, I telephoned earlier.'

'Oh, yes, Mr. Preston, I have your reservation.'

She turned to a rack on the wall, removed a buff-coloured envelope and handed it to me. Inside was a long pale green ticket.

'Hey, this is round trip,' I exclaimed.

'That's correct. Shortly after you

telephoned, we received a cancellation from San Francisco and I was able to book you on the ten-thirty return flight.'

If only a man could keep his eyes closed and form his own picture of the shape that must go with that voice, the world would be a happier place. I thanked her and made my way out to the tarmac. They were calling out the flight route of the plane I wanted. A trim little miss in the black uniform with the orange lapels marked my name off her list, and I put her down on mine as I climbed up and inside. Some of the other passengers looked as they'd been travelling quite a while already. San Diego was the end of the line, and they were probably fretting at having a stopover just an hour short of their destination. Still, it was cabin class, and if you want the reduced price on the tickets, you have to settle for bus-ride techniques. The guy sitting next to me was slumped back in his seat. He was unlovely as he slept, but I was thankful not to have to have a travel pest for company. Within about ten minutes we were moving.

On the way I thought about Doctor Petersen, the man I was aiming to contact. I knew I was taking a long chance by trying to see him personally. The smart thing to do would have been to telephone his hotel and try to arrange an appointment. I'd considered that, but decided that it was an easy matter for an efficient secretary to get rid of people on the other end of a telephone. I could imagine Petersen as a busy man, and certainly an important one. He wouldn't have time to talk to one in five of the people who wanted to see him about a hundred different things. I was hoping that a surprise call by someone who wanted to talk about a newly-dead friend might just tip the scale in my favour. An hour is not a long time when you're busy thinking. I peeked at my watch as we taxied along the runway towards the debarking point at San Diego Airport. It said eight-fifteen, and five minutes later I was trying to remember some of the football plays I once knew, as everybody jostled for cabs. I got one finally. The jockey said in a tired voice,

'Where to, mister?'

'The Mowbray Hotel. And — '

He held up a hand as we moved off.

'I know. Hurry it up. All the time, hurry it up.'

He treated me to a monologue on the evils of modern haste, other road-users, the hydrogen bomb and a flock of other subjects. For all his grumbling, I noticed that nothing passed us on the highway into town. The guy could drive. The Mowbray Hotel is a couple of miles outside the town, and is a well-known spot for those who want quiet and luxury. At a price, of course. It's especially handy for those travelling by air, because you don't lose any time getting snarled up in traffic. We drew up at the huge entrance. I gave the hackie an extra five and he promptly handed over his business card, which I stuck in my pocket and forgot immediately.

I went through the doors, spotted the bar and walked across the deep pile carpeting. Nobody paid me any attention. There wasn't any reason why they should. The bar was busy, mostly with people who looked as though they were having just one or two drinks before going in to dinner. I ordered Scotch on the rocks. When it came, I said to the barkeep, 'A great friend of mine is a guest here, Dr. Cosmo Petersen.'

'Oh, yes, sir, I know Dr. Petersen.'

I took out my billfold and opened it.

'I'd like to send him up a bottle of champagne. Could you arrange that?'

'With pleasure, sir. Would you like to make your selection?'

He handed over a folded card, listing the wines in the hotel cellar. I flicked my eyes down it.

'Number thirty-four, please.'

'Yes, *sir*,' he replied, with enthusiasm.

I put some bills on the counter, enough over the price of the champagne to ensure a little service. The barkeep walked to the other end of the counter and waved a hand. A slight kid in a bellhop's uniform detached himself from his station by the doorway and threaded his way through the customers. I swallowed the rest of the Scotch and went back into the foyer. There I sat in a hard chair close by the

137

elevators. Five minutes later the bellhop appeared, carrying a silver tray complete with ice bucket, topped by a slender black bottle-neck featuring plenty of gold wire. He crossed to the elevators and pushed a button. The red lights on the wall above glowed briefly in each of the floor indicators and finally stopped. The doors slid open and the kid stepped inside. I was a yard behind him. As soon as I was inside, the kid said,

'Excuse me, sir,' and walked out again.

'Don't get out on account of me, son.'

'Regulations, sir. We're not allowed to inconvenience the guests. I can easily wait for the next elevator.'

I grinned in my most friendly way. I could have strangled him.

'No need,' I said. 'Come on back. What floor do you want?'

'Eight,' he said.

'Well, fine,' I replied. Then turning to the elevator man, 'Seven, please.'

He hadn't said a word all along, just stood impassively by his control panel. Now he got busy with his switches and we were away. At the seventh floor we glided to a stop. I stepped out, said thanks, and winked at the bellhop. As the doors closed soundlessly, I headed for the stairway and made fast time up the carpeted treads. I reached the eighth floor just as the elevator started on its downward journey. The bellhop was turning a corner. I shot after him and poked my head round. He stopped outside one of the white doors, and tapped discreetly. I got back to the stairs and walked down one flight, waiting. A couple of minutes ticked by, then I heard the sound of the elevator going up. Somebody spoke, I couldn't catch the words, then I heard it going down again. I walked back up the stairs with a little more reserve than last time, and made my way to the door I wanted. I tapped on it. After a while it opened, and a man stood looking at me. He was between thirty and thirty-five, with a worried, pinched face. He didn't speak.

'I'd like to see Dr. Petersen for a few minutes.'

That didn't exactly seem to surprise him.

'Half the people in the country would

like to do that. What's your claim to fame?'

The voice was dry and brittle, the attitude uncompromising.

'I want to talk about a great personal friend of the Doctor's who died recently. His name was Benedict Van Huizen.'

He looked even more worried than before.

'Newspaper man?'

I shook my head.

'No, I'm an investigator from the insurance company which carried Mr. Van Huizen's cover for a very large sum.'

'Oh. Come inside.'

He stood back to allow me room to get by. I stepped in and he shut the door. I'll never know how he did it, but the next thing I knew my right arm was locked half-way up my back and strong fingers were reaching inside my coat. He gave a little grunt as he found the .38 and plucked it out. My arm was released and I had the pleasure of staring down the black snout of my own gun. He jerked it towards a door. I shrugged and went through the door.

It was a large room. At the far side a man sat at a small table writing. He looked up briefly, then carried on with what he was doing. The ice bucket with the champagne in it lay on the floor. Dr. Cosmo Petersen, if that was the man at the table, was a little round character with apple cheeks and wild white hair. I've seldom seen a man with more good humour stamped all over him. Nobody said anything until finally he pushed his papers away from him. Then he had a look at me, dark eyes twinkling beneath the bushy white brows.

'So you were right, Alex.'

The guy with my gun in his paw shrugged. Petersen beamed.

'Alex was expecting you, my friend. As soon as that came,' he jabbed a finger towards the ice bucket, 'Alex said it was undoubtedly a stratagem to learn the number of my room.'

'What's all the rough stuff about?' I enquired. 'I only came to ask you a few questions.'

'I took this from under his arm,' commented Alex, waving the .38.

'So. Do you always call on people with one of those?'

'Look, Doctor, we've got off on the wrong foot here. You misunderstand me entirely.'

I was beginning to feel uncomfortable. The rest of the party, however, seemed to be having a good time. Alex said,

'He claims to be an investigator from the insurance company that covered Mr. Van Huizen.'

'Ah,' another twinkle. 'Now that was bad luck. A few hours ago I'd have believed that, but unfortunately a real investigator from that company was here only this afternoon.'

It certainly didn't seem to be one of my lucky nights. Petersen talked on.

'I must say that when the Navy insisted on providing me with protection I didn't take it very seriously. These threats and so on,' he shrugged his shoulders, 'I regarded as the work of a few cranks. I am very grateful to the Navy, and to you personally, Alex. From the look of this young man, I'd say he was rather more of a handful than I could manage.'

'At your service, Doctor. I'd better get this guy locked up. We can think of a charge later.'

Alex walked to where an ivory telephone rested on a small table. I said,

'Before you pick that up, let me tell you who I am. The name is Mark Preston. I'm from Monkton City. In my pocket there's a licence permitting me to accept inquiries as a private investigator.'

'So what? Even if your identification is genuine, it's no guarantee you didn't come here to kill Doctor Petersen.'

That was true enough to make me think a little harder. Like most people engaged in public work of real importance, Petersen would be the natural target for a number of organisations which, for one reason or another, didn't want his work to succeed. I'd have to do better than identify myself.

'My political record will stand any investigation. I admit I used the champagne trick to find out where the Doctor was. If I'd asked for him at the reception desk, I'd have been told he was out. Isn't that right, Dr. Petersen?' I turned to him.

143

'Well, I must admit, er, probably. So many people want to see me, you know.'

'Exactly. My business is personal and urgent. I haven't travelled clear from Monkton City to waste your time.'

'Even if you are what you say, why tell a lie about being an insurance man?'

'Because the questions I want answered might be regarded by you as highly confidential. You might have talked to an official where you wouldn't to a private cop.'

Alex was standing by the telephone, listening carefully. The .38 didn't waver at all. It was my estimate that I'd take the slugs about one inch below the heart if I so much as sneezed at the wrong time. Petersen studied me, then looked across at his private army.

'What do you think, Alex?'

'I think he's unarmed and I have this,' Alex tapped the automatic. 'I think talking costs nothing and if you wish to let him talk, Doctor, I have no objection. So long as you don't get between us, of course,' he added.

'Of course. Well, there you are, Mr.

144

Preston. If you still want to talk to me, we can always lock you up afterwards.'

Petersen smiled at me cheerfully, his round face splitting into benevolent creases. I felt better. Even if I was going to be dragged off for some pointless questioning, at least there'd be some talk first. Maybe I'd even find out what I wanted to know.

'Could I smoke?' I asked.

'No.' Alex answered before Petersen had a chance. 'No smoking, no drinking, no shenanigans with the hands at all. Just keep 'em still and in plain view.'

I was mildly relieved that I really was a casual visitor. It didn't seem to me anybody was going to pull much stuff while Alex was around. The guy was good. I got on with the programme.

'Doctor, you knew Van Huizen well, I hear. How well?'

The little round man sat down.

'His father and I were at college together. I guess you might say I've known Ben since birth.'

'I see. He came to visit you here last Wednesday, I believe?'

The bushy eyebrows elevated one-half inch.

'How do you know that?'

'A lady told me. Is it true?'

'A lady,' he said the word musingly, as though pondering its accuracy. 'It wasn't Marcia. She didn't know.'

'So I understand.'

'Then it was the other one, the one from San Francisco,' he announced.

It surprised me a little.

'You know about her?' I queried.

'Oh, yes. Ben told me the story. Not her name, of course. It worried him that he had to live that kind of life.'

It had been my intention to keep Rona Parsons out of this conversation, but it looked as though I'd been beaten to the draw by the late lamented.

'So long as you know she exists, I can talk more freely. She's the one who paid my fare. She doesn't believe Van Huizen shot himself. She thinks he was murdered.'

'Ah,' he muttered softly, 'I see. When Ben told me about this woman, I imagined the picture he painted to be strongly influenced by his natural desire to speak well of her. It seems I owe her an apology. You say she hired you?'

'She's convinced it was murder. If it can be proved, it takes the smear of suicide off his name. That's what she wants.'

'She sounds like a remarkable young woman. It's a pity Ben — well, never mind that now. How can I help you?'

'After his visit to you, Van Huizen went off his food for a couple of days. Why?'

Petersen bounced up out of his chair and paced about, deep in thought. The only sound was the quiet shushing of his feet on the carpeted floor. Alex didn't take his eyes off me. Suddenly the Doctor stopped pacing and faced me squarely.

'I'm afraid you've had a wasted journey, Mr. Preston. There's no doubt in my mind that Ben killed himself. He had a cardiac condition, that's why he came to see me last week. He'd known for some time there was something wrong with him, but didn't dare to consult a local physician. There was some business deal or other in progress. Ben felt he couldn't trust anybody but me to examine him.'

'And what did you find, Doctor Petersen?'

'I'll spare you the six-syllable words. A regrettable trait among certain of the lesser men in my profession is to wave their doubtful qualifications in the faces of laymen. You may accept it that I am qualified to pass a professional opinion. Ben Van Huizen would have died within six months at the most.'

It was a bad shock. I'd been busy with a dozen jigsaw puzzles since the day before. They all had the same characters, but each picture presented a different composition. The only thing them all had in common with each other was the murdered body of Benedict Van Huizen. And here in a quiet hotel room, miles away from all the concerned parties, I stood quietly in front of a gun held by a Naval Security man who knew which part was the trigger, while an elderly doctor kicked my pieces all round the room. I knew better than to ask a man like Petersen whether he was sure of his facts. I knew he was. Instead I asked him,

'Did he know? I mean, did you tell him?'

The white head bobbed up and down.

'I'd known him all his life. He came to me only once as a doctor. All that I could tell him was that he was a dying man. It wasn't an enviable moment for either of us, Mr. Preston.'

'I guess not, sir.' I could see the little doctor was choked up. 'Tell me, in your opinion was he the type of man who'd take his own life?'

He started at me vaguely.

'What type of man would that be? I am not a psychoanalyst, Mr. Preston. If you mean was he highly strung, emotional, a chronic sufferer from nervous complaints, the answer is no. But don't set too much store by what I've said. When Ben visited me last Wednesday, he was a man I'd known since the cradle. I could have predicted with confidence exactly what he would do under a given set of circumstances. When he left here he was a stranger to me, a man I'd never seen before. A man who'd just had a death sentence pronounced on him. That man might do almost anything and not surprise me at all. And,' he paused meaningly, 'he is dead, isn't he?'

'I see what you mean.'

My feet were getting uncomfortable, standing in one position such a long time. I shifted my weight. Instantly Alex stiffened.

'Take it easy, Alex. You must have heard enough by now to convince even you,' I told him.

'Not quite. Name an official in Monkton who'll give you a clean bill,' was his reply.

I pretended to give it thought.

'Police Headquarters. Get Rourke, the man in charge of the Homicide Bureau.'

He picked up the receiver and muttered into it. I addressed Petersen again.

'Doctor, you've been co-operative, and I appreciate it. Could you tell me one more thing? From what I can make of it, Van Huizen was a clean-living man. How come he got his private life in such a mess? And I am talking about his women.'

'I'm sorry, Preston, I can't discuss that

with you. The person best qualified to do that is still very much alive. I suggest you approach her.'

His tone was quite final. I wouldn't get any place trying to persuade him to change his mind.

'Marcia?'

He nodded.

'I only had the pleasure of meeting the lady once. It was not an acquaintanceship I was anxious to continue.'

'I see.'

Alex said.

'Well, thank you, Lieutenant. If we can do something for you some time — . Sure. Goodbye.'

He replaced the phone on the hook and said to me,

'All right, Preston, let's have a look at it.'

I grinned and slipped off my jacket. Petersen watched in amazement while I rolled up my left shirt sleeve. Alex stared at the scarred, criss-crossed flesh.

'O.K., I guess you're in.'

The little doctor butted in.

'I hope you won't think I'm being

over-curious, but precisely what is going on?' He sounded like an aggrieved school kid.

'Identification, Doctor. The best kind there is. Personal body marks. Preston here was doing a little job of work for Uncle Sam when he picked up those souvenirs.'

'War wound?' queried Petersen. When I nodded, the bright eyes clouded over. 'Ah, yes, they were bad days. I'm sorry about your arm.'

He sounded as though he really meant it.

'It was years ago, Doctor. It doesn't give me any trouble now. And,' I cracked, 'it does come in handy for getting me off the hook sometimes. Such as now.'

'Nothing personal, Preston. I have a job to do, that's all.'

When I looked, I found that the gun was no longer pointing at me. I thought I might risk a cigarette now. Alex had another name. It was Baynard. We chatted for a while about harmless things. Petersen didn't say a lot. I told them I had a plane to catch at ten-thirty.

Baynard looked at his watch.

'Might take a ride out there with you myself. Doctor, would you object if I took Preston out to the airport? Danielli could take over here till I get back.'

Petersen hardly seemed to have heard. He was standing by a row of books, staring at the titles. I didn't think he was reading them. Suddenly it dawned on him that he was expected to make a contribution.

'Eh? Oh, surely. Yes, by all means. You go right ahead, Alex. No place for a young man anyhow, cooped up with an old duffer like me.'

Ten minutes later we left the suite. A large, capable-looking character had arrived to pinch-hit as watchdog. A unobtrusive sedan waited at the bottom of the steps in front of the hotel. Baynard spoke to the kid at the wheel, motioning him out.

'O.K., Ted, I won't be needing you. I'll be back in a little over an hour.'

Then he slid behind the wheel, leaning over to unlock the passenger door so that I could get in. As we moved on to the highway I observed.

'The good doctor kind of dried up there towards the end. Was it something I said?'

Baynard swerved hard to avoid a heap of tins with an engine underneath and a dozen rowdy high-school kids on top. He delivered an opinion or two about hot rods, kids in general and the like, before answering me.

'It was your arm. It reminded him of the war. He doesn't like to remember it too often. He lost two sons in the Pacific theatre, and his daughter was killed in a bombing raid on England.'

After that there didn't seem to be a lot to say. He was a good driver and I had fifteen minutes in hand when I slid out at the terminal entrance. I stuck my hand through the window.

'So long, Baynard. Look after the old guy.'

His hand was firm. Then he dived in his pocket and produced my automatic.

'You may need this some time.'

I waved him off and made my way to the airport bar for one drink before going aboard. I wasn't so lucky with my fellow passenger this time. I'd drawn a large Mexican woman who overflowed comfortably into a good proportion of my seat. She beamed at me with high good humour. Wedged solidly on her ample lap was a vast wicker basket from which floated strange odours. By the time we were half-way to Monkton City, I'd planned a foolproof smuggling scheme. Close contact with the basket had taught me one thing. The customs' man who would dig his hands into the evil-smelling contents hadn't been born. All you had to do was line the bottom of the basket with — well, anyway it helped pass the time. When the lighted notice over the door to the crew cabin flashed on, I put out my cigarette thankfully. A few minutes later I unbuckled the belt and made for the door. I was first in line. The hostess was a well-built girl with sandy hair and tired eyes.

'I don't know how you managed to stick it out,' she whispered. 'Even back here I had to keep using eau-de-Cologne.'

I winked at her and made a dive for the open hatch. There I stood, taking in deep draughts of good clear air. It was a quarter of twelve midnight when I unlocked the door of my car. A patrolling airport cop stopped and took a long look at me as I got in and roared the motor. As I passed the lighted entrance hall I saw my late travelling companion staggering along under the weight of the basket. It was odd how deep a traffic lane she left among the people around her. I'd quit worrying about the contents by the time I entered the Parkside Towers.

'Oh, Mr. Preston.'

It was Joe, the night man. He turned down the paper back he'd been reading.

'Your friend got here about thirty minutes ago. I gave him your key like you said.'

So Hillier had been early. At least I wouldn't have to wait for him.

'O.K., thanks. Anybody else ask after me, Joe?'

He shook his head.

'No, sir. Not since I came on. And Frank didn't leave me any message.'

Frank was the regular day man.

'Thanks again. G'night.'

I went up in the elevator. It had been on the tip of my tongue to ask Joe for some dope on the girl who had recently moved into the apartment next to mine. Rumour had it that she was something sensational in the way of leggy models and my curiosity was certainly piqued. Still, rumour never has it any other way. She was probably an ex-female wrestler, with muscles. There was no light under her door as I walked down the corridor. A broad strip of yellow showed under mine. I wondered what it was that brought Mr. Dean Willman Hillier careering all the way down here at midnight. My visitor had fixed the door lock so I could get in without knocking. He was sitting on an easy chair with a bottle of my best Scotch on the floor beside him. A half-empty glass rested in his left hand. His right was full of a heavy service revolver which was pointing in the general direction of my stomach. I'd never seen him before.

'Shut the door,' he commanded, 'gently.'

6

I shut the door gently.

'Who're you?' I asked.

He waved the gun. From his casual attitude I had a feeling he wasn't going to use it unless I forced him into it.

'Later. First, you come right inside and sit down. There.'

I took the chair indicated and had a good look at him. I didn't think he was very tall, maybe five eight, though you can't be sure when a man's sitting down. He was slightly built with fair hair brushed straight back. The face wasn't bad looking once you got around the little moustache, but his eyes were ice chips. I pegged him at twenty-five or six. The tuxedo he was rumpling so carelessly in the chair had set him back a hundred and fifty bucks. His voice was gentle, but that didn't mean a thing. The revolver made the difference.

'O.K., you'll know me next time. I

came here to talk.' I pointed to the weapon.

'That does plenty of talking where I come from. What do you want?'

'I'm looking for somebody. Maybe you can help me find him. I think you can.'

'Who is it?'

'There was a girl murdered here yesterday. A redhead, name of Cheryl Vickers. Does it mean anything?'

It wouldn't be any use playing completely dumb. I had to know something or the guy wouldn't be here.

'It might,' I admitted.

'Good. I want to know the name of the man who killed her. Do you know it?'

If the circumstances had been different, I might have been tempted to laugh. The casual way this character went about his questioning was not in accordance with the rules. There were two reasons I didn't laugh, and only one of them was the gun. The other was that despite the casual nature of the words, and of the man's tone, there was an air of resolve about him that was chilling. I knew that if I'd replied conversationally that I'd killed

Cheryl Vickers myself, he would just as casually have emptied that big revolver into me right where I sat.

'No, I don't. What makes you so sure I'm interested?'

He grinned, without warmth. It didn't make me feel cheerful at all.

'You did, peeper. You already told half the people in 'Frisco you're interested in the girl.'

That little offering told me two things. The first was that one of my hooks had drawn a bite. I'd had a strong feeling about San Francisco from the start of this caper. I'd left lines down in half the eateries in town, not to mention one Rona Parsons, who still featured as an interesting party, client or no client. The other thing I'd learned was that my visitor was not a native of that fair city. You never hear the home-grown product talk about 'Frisco. Always San Francisco.

'All right, so I'm interested. What makes that your business?'

The grin disappeared as though somebody had flicked a switch.

'This does,' he indicated the gun. 'And

one other thing. She was my sister. That ought to give you a pretty good idea where I stand. I'm gonna find the guy who did it, then I'm gonna kill him. I'm gonna kill anybody who tries to get in the way, too. Savvy?'

'Plenty. If you're really her brother, you're taking the wrong line with me. Put the heater in some shady spot, then maybe we can talk. I'm trying to find out about your sister's death myself.'

He watched me closely as I spoke. When I'd finished, he thought it over. Finally he shrugged, stuck the gun inside the waistband of his pants.

'Fine,' I said. 'Have you been to the cops?'

He laughed mirthlessly.

'I want this guy dead. I don't want his firearms permit revoked. I don't want some high-priced lawyer shouting about brutal District Attorney's men intimidating his client, so finally the guy winds up with two to five.' He dropped his voice, each word a knife edge, 'I don't even want him walking that last mile, with a priest an' all. I want to do it myself. My way.'

It was comforting reflection for me that I'd had nothing to do with Cheryl Vickers' death. This guy meant business. Aloud I said,

'So we have the jump on the law. You know who Cheryl was, where she came from, what kind of friends she had. The boys at headquarters don't know anything about her at all. You willing to help me if I help you?'

He raised a hand in a gesture of hopelessness.

'What can I lose? May as well tell you, Preston, I didn't have any idea where to start when I came to this town. Your name is my only lead so far. How'd you get wise to the Irishman's, anyhow?'

The Irishman's could only be the hash joint owned by Tinplate Terence O'Neill.

'I didn't really. It was a shot in the dark.'

I told him about the part-burnt match I'd found in an ashtray in Cheryl's apartment. It wasn't the moment to mention that her dead body was in the place at the time. He whistled.

'So you dropped the word around that

you were looking for Cheryl — '

'To see what would happen,' I finished for him. 'And here you are.'

He slapped his knee and looked almost pleased. Only his eyes were still without animation.

'That's good. That's pretty damned good. I like it. Here's me riding in here like Jesse James thinking what a big surprise you're gonna get, and there's you waiting for me all the time.'

'Not exactly. On a thing like this you just wander around from one unlikely place to another. Here and there you drop your name and talk a little too loud. If you're lucky, somebody does something about you.'

He rolled up off the chair, pulling his jacket down when he stood. Then he took a pack of cigarettes from his pocket, threw one to me and lighted his own from a silver lighter.

'The name is Morley. They call me Denver on account that's where I come from. I been around California two, three years now. I gamble. Ponies, cards, the iron men, anything with a kick. I don't work for a syndicate or any of that stuff. Strictly a loner, and strictly on the up and up.'

'I've heard the name before.'

It was true. Somebody had once told me a bit about the man who was now telling me his story. I'd never heard anything special about him, except that he would place ten coarse notes on the oldest plug at the track if he felt it was his lucky day.

'Cheryl stayed behind in Colorado. Then when I started operating around this area six, eight months ago, she hopped on the first thing on wheels.'

'Hollywood?' I needn't have asked.

He nodded grimly.

'What is it with these dames? Nearly forty years now since they started heading this way. Not one in five hundred even gets inside the gates of a major studio. Will they ever learn?'

It didn't need an answer. You could hear the same conversation taking place any day in any bar within a hundred miles of Faketown, which is what we call Hollywood.

'So she came. I couldn't stop her coming, but I could play the heavy when she got here. I know 'Frisco, L.A., all of 'em. I know the phoney agents and the photo fakes and the screen test brigade. I put Cheryl to regular work in a decent place where I knew somebody could keep an eye on her when I wasn't around. A fighter's hangout. Not very elegant maybe, but nobody pulls any stuff around the Irishman's, not when the word is out.'

He passed a hand across his face, as though trying to shut off a view of something.

'I tried to keep her in line, honest to God. Then a few weeks ago she started acting very chirpy. We hadn't been getting along too well, what with me keeping tabs on her and all. She told me there was somebody else interested in her besides me, a big local name. She wouldn't tell me who it was. Then last week, Friday, she disappeared. Just packed a grip and disappeared, while I was out seeing to a little business. Next thing I knew was when I picked up the paper this morning.'

Morley turned away slightly so I

couldn't see his face. I didn't want to anyway. It wasn't hard to imagine the way he was feeling. I got myself a glass and picked the Scotch up off the floor. Splashing some into his empty tumbler, I handed it to him.

'Kinda chilly in here,' I said. 'Try this.'

He gulped at the stuff, then breathed very deeply before speaking again.

'I came over right away, but I didn't know where to start. I'd told the Irishman I'd call him up and give him my address when I knew it. I did that tonight, he told me about you, and here I am.'

It fitted together well. I said,

'And then when you got here, the porter gave you the key to my apartment because he knew I was expecting somebody.'

'Right. How about that anyway? Nobody else showed so far.'

It was the first time I'd remembered Hillier since I got back. He'd probably decided that whatever it was could keep until morning.

'Maybe he changed his mind.' I took another measure from the bottle, then sat

166

down again. 'This guy she mentioned, why wouldn't she tell you his name?'

'Two reasons, I guess. One was that she figured I'd probably go and rough him up. She was right about that. The other one I couldn't figure at first till I got to thinking about it. She told me the guy was mixed up in some business deal, and couldn't afford any publicity for a while. I thought that sounded phoney at the time, but I couldn't put my finger on it.'

'But you've got it licked now?'

'I think so, yeah. I think maybe there was really some kinda deal cooking. Why the guy couldn't stand the flash-bulbs was because he was already married. If he was a business guy, anything like that might give his credit a jolt.'

'Yes,' I replied musingly. 'Could be you're right, at that.'

'This was supposed to be a two-way conversation, right? How about you kicking in with your end. What makes all of this any of your put-in?'

I'd already decided two things. Cheryl's brother was entitled to some kind of a break, and in the second place I thought he could be trusted. To a point.

'You ever hear of a man named Benedict Van Huizen?'

Morley screwed up his face, repeating the name softly.

'The financier? Yeah, I got him. Don't tell me he figures in this.'

'The only place he figures any more is out at the Sleep Softly Gardens. The man is dead. Since Tuesday night.'

'Tuesday? I don't get it. Cheryl died Tuesday night, sure, but where's the connection?'

I finished the last of my drink before answering.

'Van Huizen killed himself around ten-thirty. He stuck a very large old-fashioned Colt revolver in his mouth and blew out his brains.'

'So?'

'So the gun he used was the same gun killed your sister.'

He stood quite still, staring at me as though unwilling to have heard what I'd said. When he spoke, the words were quiet but very distinct. And he had that look in his eyes again.

168

'You're telling me what, exactly?'

'I'm telling you facts, Morley. Facts that are a matter of police record. No guess-work from me.'

He went and sat down stiffly, perching on the edge of a chair as though he might leap up and rush out suddenly.

'You mean this big shot and Cheryl? You're crazy.' He punched his fist angrily into the soft arm of the chair. 'This Van Huizen, why, he was somebody. Guys like that don't go around killing girls. They got dough, lots of it. A girl finds herself in a little trouble. Those guys buy it off quiet. Everything peaceful and the girl taken care of. I've seen it done.'

I hadn't got any argument to offer. I'd seen it done myself. I said,

'Can't you think of anything she said that would give you any idea at all that she tied in with Van Huizen?'

'I already told you what she said. The guy was a big name around — ' He broke off in the middle, as though just making sense of the words. Then, in a hurry for me to contradict him, he rushed on. 'But there was this talk of a deal. Something

169

important. That leaves Van Huizen out, no?'

'No,' I shook my head slowly. 'No, it doesn't leave him out. It puts him where the blue chips go. The man was negotiating some very large merger. Not a little affair, something involving his whole combine.'

Morley's face was drained of colour now, except the cold green of his eyes. When he spoke he no longer had the firm control on his voice. Gun or no gun, he was a guy whose sister had been shot down only twenty-four hours before, and he was taking it pretty hard.

'So this is the way it reads? This Van Huizen killed her, then himself. That right?'

'I've only told you what the boys at headquarters have entered on their files.'

Interest flickered momentarily on his face.

'You're trying to tell me something. What is it?'

'Van Huizen left a widow, Marcia. She doesn't go for this murder and suicide at all.'

He laughed shortly.

'Oh, she doesn't huh? If the lawmen figure it that way, they got their reasons. What I hear tell, these Monkton coppers are a square team.'

'That's true, and I wish a certain friend of mine named Rourke had heard you say that. Trouble is the Van Huizen end is not City business. His house is way outside the City limits. And that means the County Sheriff's office.'

'Go on,' he was hanging on to every word I said.

'They arrived at this conclusion last night. But you caught the morning editions — '

'And the afternoon. And tonight's. What about it?'

'You would have noticed if any progress was reported about catching up with the killer.'

He drew in his breath, and the air sighed softly over his teeth.

'Say, that's right. There wasn't a word. Not a word. Listen,' he was getting more animated all the time. 'If anybody thinks they're going to smooth this over just because the guy had millions, they got another think coming.' He passed a hand across his furrowed forehead. 'But his wife, this Marcia, you say she don't go for it. Why?'

I shrugged.

'Beats me. And that's where I come in. She's retained me to look this over — Cheryl, her husband, the gun, the whole bit. She says it stinks.'

'I'll go along with that.'

He sat quietly, thinking. I didn't interrupt him. I thought the version I'd given Morley put us all in a better light, and saved me from questions I wouldn't want to answer. The blackmail stuff would only upset the gambler, and anyway I'd have had to be thinking pretty fast to avoid telling him more, especially the part about me finding Cheryl's body. I'd had a long day, and a long journey at the end of it. It was open to doubt whether I could think fast enough to wriggle round all the corners. John Rourke was a good friend of mine, but if he found out I'd failed to report a homicide, it would mean my licence.

Suddenly Morley came back at me sideways.

'This County Sheriff's outfit. Who handles from there?'

'Man named Harrigan. He's smart, a little bit tough, and can even get mean if he has to. But he deals them off the top.'

'You sure about him?'

'I'm sure.' I meant it.

'How about the top man? The People's Choice?'

'Name of Savage. Not a regular politician. He was area representative for Coastal and Amalgamated Insurance for years. Then I guess the bug got him and he got on the gravy train at the last election.'

'You know anything about him?' queried Morley.

What did I know about Savage? I pictured him as I'd last seen him. A square-faced, unpleasant-looking man of forty-five to fifty. Coastal had the cover for a plateful of gems that some of the citizens had removed from a movie director's house at Copra Bay. I'd had a talk with the new owners, then a lot more talk with Coastal. Finally I met Savage in a hotel a hundred miles from Monkton. He handed me fifteen thousand dollars and I handed him a bagful of ice worth ten times that. It wasn't a fair meeting on which to judge a man. He didn't exactly work up a sweat trying to make me feel at home, but there was no reason why he should love me. Maybe he thought it was me organised the heist. It wasn't. I got five hundred bucks and the money for my plane ticket.

'I only met him a few times. I didn't like his face. He didn't care for mine either.'

'Uh huh.' Morley stifled a yawn. 'Well, where do we go from here?'

'Tonight, we don't go anywhere. Except bed. Take it easy. I may not be the best in the world, but I do get results now and then. After all, you came out of nowhere, didn't you? Within a few hours. Let's sleep on it, see what gives tomorrow.'

'Maybe you're right.' He got up. 'I'm staying at the Terreno Hotel if you want me.'

'O.K.' I walked with him to the door.

'Are you going to the police?'

'I don't know. Maybe, I'll see. Me and those boys don't get along too well, in the usual run. This is kind of different, but — ' he heaved his shoulders. 'Well, I don't know. If anything breaks, you'll call me?'

'Sure. And, Morley — '

He turned in the hallway. 'Yeah?'

'I'm sorry about your sister.'

'Yeah.'

He stuck his hands in his pockets and walked away, head sunk low on his chest. I went back inside and shut the door. The phone rang as I was reaching for the bottle. That would be Hillier.

'Preston,' I muttered into the mouthpiece.

'Hey, Mark, boy, thassa you? Where you been? Two times I phone already.'

Not Hillier. It was Bonnie Anselmo.

'Sure it's me. Who else? And I've been out of town tonight.'

'Oh. Listen, Mark. That party you mention to me thees afternoon. I seen him.'

I was interested, fast. George Porter

had been postponed because of my urgent trip to San Diego. I was plenty concerned about Porter and had intended to start combing the town next morning.

'Where was this?' I queried.

'In the street. I went uptown to see my poor cousin, Manuelo. Say, he's a pretty seeck that Manuelo. Alla over hees face is big lumps. I tole hees mother, you watcha thees boy — '

'That's tough, about Manuelo. I hope he recovers real fast. A good boy. About Porter — '

'Sure, sure, I'm a just comin' to heem. Well, after I leava the house, who'sa right there on the sidewalk?'

'George Porter?'

'Sure. Say, hee's all dressed up like a T'anksgiving dinner. I give heem the big hello, you know, and whaddya teenk 'e say?'

'Knowing what a sweet guy he is, I'd say he gave you a fast goodbye.'

'It'sa true. 'E say, 'Ho It'sa you. Well you don't catcha George Porter in no wop dumps. This oughta pay you off permanent.' Then he geev me fifty bucks.

I tella heem where to put hees money, but I don'ta want no trouble outside a my own cousin's house. How you like that bum, Mark?'

George Porter, all neat and tidy, and handing out fifty dollar bills. I wasn't tired any more.

'I don't like him, Bonnie. But I gotta see him. Did you find out if he's back at the Hacienda?'

'Sure. I check on it. Number 307. And say, Mark, you gonna have maybe a li'l argument with thees Porter?'

'It could work out that way.'

'Well, you geev him one for Anselmo. And make it low down, huh?'

'Sure. About the fifty, did you see his roll?'

A whistling came out of the earpiece and nearly split my head.

'See it? I shoulda say. Thees Porter, he rob the bank sure.'

'Thanks a lot for letting me know, Bonnie, I appreciate it.'

He told me the story again, but there was nothing the second time I hadn't heard the first time. Finally I was able to finish it off. I made another call, waited a long time for an answer, then got a sleepy 'Hallo'. It took me a full minute to wake the guy up, then six more of hard talking to convince him. When I was through, I checked my pockets, flicked out the lights and left the apartment.

★　★　★

The trap was called the Blue Lagoon, and the guy who thought that one up was either dumb or a wag. The furnishings were faded and the paint-work chipped and stained. I took an imported beer because that comes in a bottle with a seal on the cap. The character behind the sticky counter looked like an extra in one of those prison movies. The rest of the company didn't inspire me any. I retired to a seat where I could watch the door. The Blue Lagoon is fifteen miles from the city and the only place along that road where a man can buy a drink of the hard stuff at two-thirty in the morning. I didn't want a drink, I wanted to go to bed, but there was something brewing in my busy little mind and there'd be no sleep for me until I'd given it a chance to work itself out.

Harrigan came in after about fifteen minutes. He didn't see me right away, and as he looked around, I noticed quite a few guys who seemed to be wishing they could hide under their chairs. When he saw me, he nodded, stopped at the bar for an order, then came over, glass in hand. His face was haggard.

'You know how much sleep I've had in two days? Less than three hours. So this had better be very, very good.' It was his idea of a greeting.

'I don't think it is. I think it's gonna be bad.' I took a pull at the beer. 'Bad for you, Harrigan.'

He inclined his head, as though the weight of it was more than a tired neck could carry.

'Bad things happen to me all the time. Usually I don't need to get out of bed to listen to them. How would it be if you told me about this one?'

'The Van Huizen thing — ' I began.

'Not that, still? You don't give up easy,

do you, Preston?'

'No, neither will you when I tell you what I'm thinking.'

'Will you for goshsakes get on with it? I'm tired. I'm getting to be an old man. Just say what you want and cut out the guessing games.'

'All right. I think they sold you out, Harrigan.' He'd told me to get it said.

His right forefinger tapped slowly on the table-top. Then he looked up at me.

'There has to be more.'

'There's more. I've heard about you over the years. Not all of it was nice, but one thing I'm fairly sure of, you're not the man to ride along with a set-up.'

He made no comment. A cop always knows when it's time to let the other fellow talk. I talked.

'So when you made your speech at Van Huizen's house last night, I accepted it. If you said suicide, O.K., it was suicide. Since then I've been thinking.'

'What about?'

'About that respected community figure, the County Sheriff.'

'That bum? Listen, Preston, if I had

any self-respect, I'd turn in my badge.'

'That's what I hear. Anything goes with Savage. Anything where that green folding stuff is involved.'

Harrigan snorted and tipped back his glass. Tears appeared in his eyes and he set the drink down hurriedly. I knew I was right about that imported beer.

'How would you like it if I told you that Benedict Van Huizen had a life cover of nearly a quarter of a million dollars? How would it sound if I threw in that his suicide would mean no bid from the insurance company?'

He wiped the moisture from his eyes with a coloured handkerchief. Methodical slow movements. He said softly,

'And this insurance company, would it have a name? A name like Coastal and Amalgamated, for instance?'

I nodded.

'Seems to me a company would be mighty pleased to find it had saved all that money. Am I talking wild, or are you still here?'

His face was grim.

'I'm still here. I didn't get the call on

this thing. I was out chasing after a stolen car. Savage booked in the report. I went along to the house as soon as I got back.'

'So some of your boys were there first?' I prompted.

'Yeah.'

He wasn't really talking to me now. He was thinking back to the night before, checking over what had happened. I thought I could try another question.

'What kind of a guy is Dunphy?'

'My deputy?' he laughed. 'A great credit to the office. Why, any politician within miles will tell you what a great guy old Tom Dunphy is. A real square guy. Square anything. Parking ticket, speeding beef, anything.'

Dunphy didn't seem to rate very high.

'Look, Preston, I wouldn't talk to you at all if this was a little thing. I'd tell you to go to hell, then I'd go back to the office and personally beat hell out of the pair of 'em. But this is the big one. I've been swallowing insults for years, putting up with fixes, contributions to the police funds, all that stuff. If you're on to something, and the way I hear it you're not a man to waste my time, then this could be the big one. What's the rest?'

'Are you running an autopsy on Van Huizen?'

'Not necessary. The cause of death was clear enough. Gunshot wound in the brain doesn't need much of a detective to spot it, huh?'

'Correct. But suppose it was murder. Suppose the killer was trying to make it look like suicide. How would he get that close? I don't know about you, but I can't see myself sitting still while somebody shoved a .45 between my teeth. Unless I was doped.'

'Doped? No,' he negatived with his head, 'that's out. I had the glass on the desk checked. Just routine, I didn't expect to find anything. Got the lab. report this morning. Good Scotch whisky, but nothing else.'

'I see. You do all these little details yourself, eh? I mean like taking a glass to the lab. boys?'

'Hell, no. Dunphy — ,' he stopped almost before he started. 'Yeah, I begin to see what you mean. Dunphy had that glass. I just thought of something else, too. If there was a killer, he'd have had to go out the window. The butler showed too quick for anybody to slip out the door. But the window was locked on the inside when inspected. And who would you think inspected it?'

I didn't have to try for that one.

'There it is, Harrigan. I don't know anything for sure, except the part about the insurance. It just occurred to me you'd be in a better position to take it from there.'

'Damn right. The more I think about it, the more I like it. Maybe I should have said the less I like it. It's a hell of a note when a police officer can't rely on the other people in his department.'

'I guess. With a little luck there may be some cleaning up now.'

I felt a little sorry for him. I've met plenty of guys like Harrigan. Career cops, honest men trying to do a decent job for a minute pay cheque, and all in the face of greedy and corrupt officials. People like to make great play about the occasional bad police officer. For every one who makes the front page in some splash about bribery or extortion, there are a hundred Harrigans plodding on, risking their lives every other day to protect the public. The same grateful public which misses no opportunity of pointing out what a bunch of crooks they are. He wasn't going to admit it to me, but I knew the lieutenant was personally grieved about Savage and Dunphy. After a silence, he said,

'What's your interest in this, Preston? I thought the dead man was your client.'

'That's right, he was. But his widow wouldn't be told it was suicide. Not even by you. She hired me to dig around. She was convinced he'd been murdered.'

He sucked at his teeth.

'Quite a girl, that one. Quite a dish, too. I remember when she came here. 'Bout three years back. Ben was a lucky guy. Somebody ought to be able to move in there and have a nice easy life.'

'Could be. Personally I don't see what would be easy about being married to a dame with that much money, especially one who looked like Marcia Van Huizen.

I'd want to know where she was every time she left the house.'

Harrigan cackled.

'Still, you got to hand it to her. She meant to get that killer caught if there was one.'

'And I say there was one. How about that autopsy? Can you arrange one without referring to Savage?'

'Sure. It's normal routine, nobody'll query my signature. If they find anything, I'll get in touch with you.'

'Fine.'

'Oh, and — Preston, I'm not going to ask questions right now, because the way I see it, you've done me a favour tonight, already. But if you feel like telling me more about this, I'll be listening. If there's anything more to tell, that is.'

I drained the last of the beer and moved the glass to the middle of the table.

'There's nothing I can tell you that's worth hearing. I have a hundred and five corners to look in, about that many people to talk to. When I get anything worth repeating you'll know.'

We shook hands outside the Blue Lagoon. The night was now turned to full cold. The moon stared blankly down from a clear black sky. I was shivering as I climbed into the heap and switched on the ignition.

When I got back to Parkside, Joe, the night porter, was standing at the top of the steps.

'Kind of late, Joe,' I remarked as I made for the door. 'You keeping awake?'

'No trouble tonight, Mr. Preston, not with the excitement and all.' He looked excited himself.

'Excitement?' He'd have been offended if I hadn't asked.

'Sure. Right after you left. Hit and run. Guy crossing the street, could have been heading right here to the Parkside. This car come out of the sky, driving like crazy. Guy never had a chance, this big sedan must have been registering seventy when it hit him.'

'Tough break,' I muttered, sympathetically.

At the door I paused, thinking. Then I released my grip on the handle and the heavy glass door swung shut. I went back to him.

'You say the victim could have been heading this way?'

He nodded, pleased to have a second chance to talk about it.

'Show me, do you mind?'

We walked down to the sidewalk. Traffic had almost finished now. He pointed out on to the roadway.

' 'Bout there was where it happened. I seen the whole thing. I'd just stepped out for fresh air — '

'Did you see the driver of the car?' I interrupted.

'No, it was all too fast for me. One second it was there, then it was gone. I had to tell the cops my story, you know.' He added importantly, 'When I get through here in the morning they want me to go down to the station and sign a statement.'

'Lucky you were around.'

'I wasn't able to do much, Mr. Preston. It was all over in a flash. You see, this guy was walking across — '

'What did he look like, the guy who was killed?'

'Well now, that's a tough one. I didn't pay him no special heed till the auto hit him. I run over at once, but he was looking different then, you bet.'

'How old would you say?'

'Forty-five. Maybe more, maybe less. Hard to say. The rear bumper must have caught his face. That's what the cops figured. They only just left ten minutes ago. Pity you didn't get back quicker than you did.'

'Yeah.'

I asked a couple more questions, but Joe was so blown up with the idea of seeing his name in the papers that he didn't contribute much in the way of answers. I knew it was just wild guessing on my part, but once I got back to the apartment, I picked up the phone. A sour male voice answered.

'Morgue.'

'Missing Persons,' I said briskly, 'you have just signed for a male cadaver, white, age forty-five. Hit and run accident at Parkside Heights. Identification complete yet?'

'Creeps, I only had the guy thirty

minutes. He'll be just as dead in the morning. You'll get the usual file report then. What's so special?'

No wonder the guy sounded peevish. Pawing over dead people in a sub-zero temperature in the middle of the night is not an easy way to earn a living.

'I'm sorry to hurry you like this,' I was very official, 'but time is very important in our present enquiries. This dead man could tie in with a Federal matter.'

And that clinched it. He gasped, and there was the sound of paper rustling.

'Say, I'm sorry, Captain. I have it right here. Identifying marks — '

'Later,' I cut in. 'Any name identification?'

'Yes. He was a George Melvin Porter.'

I could feel tiny cold things crawling up my back.

7

It was three-forty in the ackemma when I cut my lights outside the Club Rendez-vous. There were still a number of cars parked outside. I took a walk around. Three of them could have been classed as large sedans. With the small flashlight from my own car, I examined all three. One was unmarked and another looked as though someone had driven a tank against its side. There was corrosion on some of the dents, and that put the damage as happening several days ago. The third car was mostly clean, too, except for a slight dent on the front fender and one or two scratches along the side. I poked the light in at the window and found the name on the licence. Benedict Van Huizen.

The bar wasn't busy. A fair-haired boy in a white jacket was complaining because the bartender wouldn't serve him. The stuff was already pouring out of his ears, anyway. A fat middle-aged woman with a tight dress that made her look ridiculous was pulling on the boy's arm and whispering to him. The guy behind the counter was doing his best to keep civil. He looked at me sadly as I flopped on to a stool.

'Make it Scotch and plain water.'

That set the kid off again.

'How come you serve this guy, huh? 'Snot even a regular client. Never seen him 'fore. How about it, huh? 'Snot fair.'

I ignored him and sipped at the drink. The restaurant was empty now and in darkness. I noticed that the man who'd been guarding the stairs was no longer on view. It puzzled me for a moment, because I was quite sure the gaming room wouldn't have shut down yet. Shortly afterwards I had the answer. Ed Newman came down the stairs followed by the watchdog. The fair boy was slumped on the counter of the bar. Newman walked up and clapped him lightly on the back.

'How are you, Bart? Having a good time?'

The boy stirred and looked up.

'Hi, Ed. Say, you're a big noise here. Tell this guy to give me a drink, will you?'

'Why certainly, Bart, certainly. Surprised at you, Murph. Don't you know this is Bart Bankhead the Third? A drink from my special bottle at once.'

'If you say so, Mr. Newman.'

The bartender reached down and took a small bottle from a drawer. The kid looked at Newman gratefully.

'Say, Ed, you know how to treat a feller. These people,' he waved a deprecating hand, 'they don't understand a man and his liquor.'

Newman smiled in a wide, friendly fashion.

'You bet. Well, there's your drink, Bart.' He picked up one of the two glasses. 'Down the hatch.'

The kid winked triumphantly at the bartender and snatched up the drink. I didn't think it was my business to tell him that the two glasses had been filled from different bottles. Nobody paid any attention to the woman, who stood by, uncertain of what to do. The pride of the Bankheads set the empty glass down and smacked his lips.

'Say, that was really — '

The watchdog caught him as he fell off the stool. Newman reached inside the white jacket and pulled out the boy's wallet.

'Fool kid,' he grumbled. He counted up the money, folded it carefully and replaced it, slipping the wallet back in its place. 'There's two hundred and seventy dollars in there. Have Mac take the kid home, and tell him I've counted what's in the wallet. It better be there when the kid goes to bed.'

'Sure, boss.' The other man staggered out, supporting the crumpled figure of Bart Bankhead the Third.

Newman turned to the woman.

'Who're you?'

'Why, I'm — just a friend,' she said nervously, fingering her purse. 'He and I got talking, and — '

'Know her?' said Newman to the bartender.

'Yes, Mr. Newman. She's been in two, three times lately. Working the place, I guess.'

Newman's face went hard. With his left hand he gripped the woman's fleshy arm. She shivered with fright.

'This is the Club Rendezvous,' he told her, the cruel fingers biting into her, 'not Crane Street. The only reason I'm not having some leather work done on your face is because it might improve it. We don't go in for cut-price hustlers.'

'Listen, mister — ' she began, but winced with pain as Newman rolled his thumb and forefinger thoughtfully over the muscle in her arm. Beads of sweat stood out on her lip.

'You take any money off that kid?' His voice was soft and enquiring.

'No, Mr. Newman, I swear — '

'All right, all right.'

Suddenly he let go of her arm. The white patches left by his fingers suffused with blood, a livid, angry colour. She rubbed nervously at the place, her eyes fixed on Newman.

'Beat it,' he told her. 'Tell your tramp friends the Rendezvous is off limits.'

'Yeah, sure, Mr. Newman. Thanks. Well — er — g'night, Mr. Newman.'

She backed away towards the door, smiling anxiously at everybody in turn. Nobody paid her any attention. When she reached the entrance, the man who'd helped Bankhead stagger outside suddenly came through. The woman gave a little shriek, and stumbled past him. Newman said,

'How are you, Preston?'

It was the first time I realised he'd even noticed me.

'Not bad, Ed. How's this deal working out?' I looked around to indicate that the deal I referred to was the Club Rendezvous.

'Fair. These things go slow at first, but now it's picking up great. You seen upstairs?'

As a question it was rhetorical, as they say. Newman knew the name of every man, woman and child who'd been up those stairs. Mine was not featured — yet.

'No. I hear you fixed it up real pretty.'

' 'Sright. C'mon, take a look.'

The watchdog hovered around in case he was needed. I could see he wasn't sure whether I was just a buddy of Newman's, or a guy being escorted upstairs to have his brains kicked in. I sympathised with Watchdog. I didn't know either. I followed Newman up and at the top he turned right, into a large room. It was empty. I heard the door click. Newman stood with his back to it.

'All right, Preston, what gives?'

He was balanced nicely on the balls of his feet. The expensive cut of the tuxedo did not conceal the fact that his body was in good shape. Here I was, all cosy in a room with a guy who had almost been a contender for the big title. Only he looked anything but pleased to see me and I didn't feel cosy at all.

'Snap it up,' he insisted. 'What're you doing here?'

'Just came in for a drink,' I told him. 'Public place, isn't it?'

'Don't be coy with me, Preston. I might break your leg, just for laughs.'

The knowledge that he could do it without half-trying didn't cheer me in the least. There was a curtained doorway on the right. I wondered how far I'd get if I made a dive for it, decided against it.

Somehow I had a feeling someone was standing behind the curtain.

'Let's stop kidding. I know Porter's been to see you. He told me he would. You're wasting your time, Preston. You won't get a nickel out of us, and I'll smash you in little pieces if you try.'

He took a step towards me. I took one back, fast.

'Us?' I queried.

'Marcia and me. Ah,' he dropped his right arm against his side. 'What the use? Go ahead and give the story to the newspapers. It won't do much harm now.'

'Tell them about you and Marcia?'

'That phases you, huh? A week ago you coulda done a lotta harm. Now,' he shrugged, 'so a few people think we weren't very nice. Falling for another guy's wife don't win a man any popularity contests. Now the guy is dead. It'll only cause a little bit of a stir. People will forget it in three months. That's what I told Porter and that's what I'm telling you. Now get out.'

He moved away from the door. I stayed where I was.

'Porter was blackmailing you over this?'

'Stop acting so innocent or I'll lose my temper. What else did he tell you?'

'He didn't tell me anything, Ed. He's dead.'

'Huh?'

I was certain now that someone stood behind the curtain. There'd been a slight movement there when I told Newman about Porter's death.

'How d'you mean, dead? Why, I only bounced the guy out of here a couple of hours ago.'

'Well, since then somebody tried bouncing him off the roadway with an automobile. He's dead as last Christmas. And he hadn't been to see me.'

'Wow.' Newman sat down. 'Wait a minute, I gotta think about this.'

I stood still letting him think about it. In my pocket was a pack of Old Favourites. Since it looked as if Newman and I wouldn't be going to war for a minute or two at least, I pulled out the pack and lit one.

'This is on the level? I mean Porter not talking to you about us?'

'On the level.'

'I must be crazy.'

He got up and started walking around. He seemed nervous again. I watched him closely.

'That makes me the world's prize chump, I guess,' he muttered. 'Why, I've been and told you the whole thing and you didn't know anything about it.'

'I wouldn't worry about it too much. Blackmail is out of my line, and I'm not that desperate to get my name in the papers.'

He nodded.

'Yeah, yeah. Still — '

'You know, Ed, if you'd had the sense to come to me about this before, maybe I could've got Porter off your back.'

'Maybe. Well, it's history now. You say a car hit him?'

I wagged my head up and down.

'Drunk driver most likely. Porter never had a chance.'

'They got the guy? I'll pay for his defence myself. I don't care if he's guilty as hell.'

'No, they haven't picked him up yet.

Tough job tracing these guys. They're usually ordinary citizens with a load on. No criminal record or anything like that.'

He didn't answer. Just sat quite still with his long legs poked out in front of him. I kept checking on the curtain. I wanted to be ready when the guy behind there made his play.

'If you're on the level about you and the lady, it won't do any harm for me to tell you that I'm working for Marcia Van Huizen.'

Newman looked up suspiciously.

'Funny she never mentioned it to me.'

'Maybe she isn't aware of it. I was at the house when she heard about her husband's death. She said she didn't go for the suicide talk. Way she saw it, the man had been murdered, and whoever did it made it look like suicide. Then they told her about this girl in town being killed with the same gun. Murder and suicide sounded a lot more reasonable.'

'So she unhired you?'

'No. She passed out when she heard about the girl, so that leaves me still working for her until she says otherwise.'

'I see. I never figured you for a cheapskate, Preston. If you think you're gonna latch on to any of Marcia's money for asking a few questions around, you're crazy. Nothing can change a suicide into a murder.'

The menace in Newman's tone was soft but dangerous.

'Stop making noises, Ed. I know how tough you are. But I'm not working for you. I'm working for her. Got a few little things to tell her, too.'

'Such as what?' He sounded disgusted.

'I won't bother you with the details. If you happen to see the lady before I do, tell her I was looking for her.'

He made no answer, and didn't try to stop me as I left. The guy behind the curtain stayed out of sight, too. The interview with Newman hadn't worked out as I'd hoped. I'd been intending to get a glimpse of the gambling set-up, and take inventory of the players. Great help to a man in my business to know who the heavy players are. At the foot of the stairs Watchdog materialised from the shadows and stood impassively while I made my way through the bar and out. The barkeep was clearing up. I told him goodnight and went through the glass doors on to the terrace. Most of the outside lighting was switched off now. My feet scrunched on the gravel as I made my way to where I'd left the car.

'Mr. Preston.'

It was a woman's voice, and I wheeled round to see Marcia Van Huizen hurrying out of the club. I waited till she caught up with me, wrapping a fur coat around her as she walked.

'Eddie says you want to see me?'

'That's right, Mrs. Van Huizen. But this is hardly the spot to talk.'

'You're right. I should freeze in about five minutes.'

I thought quickly.

'At this hour there aren't any spots open in town. Would you mind if we went to my place?'

She wasn't a girl to waste time when she was cold. At once she said.

'All right. I've got a car here. You lead the way.'

Then she was off among the parked

203

cars. I climbed into mine, gunned the motor and switched on the lights. More lights sprang up away on my left. As I rolled out of the entrance, the twin spots took up their place in my rear mirror and hung there until we reached Parkside. When Marcia drew up, I walked up and stuck my head in the window.

'Give me one minute to get rid of the porter. That'll save you being embarrassed or recognised.'

'Or both,' she said with a chuckle.

Inside I gave Joe five dollars to go comb his hair. I guess being a night porter teaches a man many things. He took the five, folded it carefully and tucked it in a small inside pocket on the waistband of his pants. Then he said thoughtfully,

'Been thinking about taking a short break. 'Bout two minutes was what I had in mind.'

'And another two when I phone from upstairs later,' I prodded.

'Sure thing, Mr. Preston. Two now and two later.' He shuffled away down a passage. Marcia appeared at the door. I let her in and led her up to the apartment.

'Well this is quite nice. Really quite nice,' she said as she stood inside the door.

'Let me take your coat,' I offered.

As the heavy fur slid from her shoulders, I caught my breath. The emerald green dress was supported by a single thin strap that passed around the back of her neck, widening slightly in an attempt to conceal at least part of her high exciting breasts. The attempt was not a complete success. At the back the material didn't even begin until somewhere close to the base of her spine. The deep suntan seemed to be even all over. The brown eyes surveyed me coolly.

'Mr. Preston, I came here to talk business. I'm sure we're both quite clear about that.'

I bowed.

'Fair comment. Could I fix a drink?'

'Not for me, thank you. I'd like a cigarette though.'

While she sat down I dug around for smokes and matches. If I was supposed to sit around and talk business to a girl who looked like she did at past four in the morning, I decided I would need a drink. While I was pouring it out, she said,

'Eddie tells me you're under the impression you are working for me, Mr. Preston.'

'That's right.' I took a sip of the Scotch and went to another chair where I wouldn't miss any of her.

'But surely you must have realised that what I'd been saying to you was cancelled out by what that man, er — '

'Harrigan,' I supplied.

'Yes, Harrigan. I mean once he came out with the news about this miserable girl's death, it rather altered things, didn't it?'

I shook my head.

'Not for me. I took five hundred dollars of your husband's money. Seems to me he — or his family — ought to be entitled to a little service for that kind of money.'

She looked faintly surprised.

'That's very admirable, if you don't mind my saying so, but a little quixotic. You yourself told me it would be a waste of time carrying on.'

'True, I did say something like that. But things have been happening. Some of them you ought to know. After I tell you, if you don't feel like hiring me, we're even.'

'And you'll drop the matter?'

'I didn't say that.'

'But surely if you're not getting paid — '

'There may be other people than yourself willing to pay to find out the truth of this thing, Mrs. Van Huizen.'

'Others? Who, for example?'

'I can't tell you that. This is a confidential business I'm in. I don't tell them about you, I don't tell you about them.'

'But if we have common interests — ?'

I interrupted her again. It was getting to be a habit.

'I didn't say you had common interests. That's not for me to judge. All I said was you are interested in the same thing. Your motives may be a mile apart for all I know. And justice may not be of special interest to any of you.'

The long slender fingers tapped fluidly on the arm of the chair.

'I begin to get an idea of what Dean meant,' she said quietly.

'Dean Hillier?' I queried. 'What he meant by what?'

'By insisting that you were the man to investigate that girl's background. The one who was bothering my husband.'

'That was Hillier's idea, huh?'

'Why, yes, originally at least.'

'Mrs. Van Huizen,' I leaned towards her, cradling the glass in my hands, 'could you tell me a little more about that? About how I came to be hired in the first place?'

She looked puzzled.

'More? Just what more is there? I mean Dean must have told you the story when he came to your office.'

'Yeah, he told me. Trouble is, I didn't ask many questions. Hillier filled in as many facts as I needed to know to get me started. Blackmail is more or less routine in my line of business. I didn't bother asking a lot of questions.'

'And now?'

'Now two people are dead,' I pointed out. 'Three, if you count a man named George Porter, and I do count him.'

'Porter? But you said he was accidentally killed by a hit-and-run driver — ' She stopped as she realised what she was saying, and some of the colour left her face.

'Did I, Mrs. Van Huizen? When did I say that? While you were hiding behind a curtain in the Club Rendezvous?'

'You have absolutely no right to question me. I refuse to be cross-examined.'

Marcia Van Huizen had that strained look again, the one I'd seen when she'd had a sight of her husband's corpse.

'That's true. I don't have any rights around here at all. You can put your pretty coat on and walk right out whenever you feel like it, lady.'

For a few moments she said nothing. I could see she was struggling with herself. There was a battle going on inside her between her anxiety to get at the truth and her annoyance with one Mark Preston, Confidential Enquiries Made,

Fees Exorbitant. All at once she seemed to relax.

'Is the offer of a drink still open, Mr. Preston?'

'You bet.'

I didn't ask what she wanted. I tipped a jigger of gin into a glass, added two drops of angostura bitters and showed the glass a piece of lemon peel. She took it firmly between the thumb and first two fingers of her right hand, and sipped. Her eyes closed and the beginning of a smile played around her mouth.

'Are you always right about what will please a woman, Mr. Preston?'

'Not always,' I confessed. 'Last month I was thrown down two flights of stairs by a lady wrestler. She didn't care for one of my holds.'

The smile was very faint, but I had a feeling I might begin to get some answers. I started the campaign.

'I'm sorry if you don't like some of my questions. I seem to have a talent for saying the wrong things to you. If I do it again, can you try to remember I'm a guy who is paid to ask questions? Lots of questions.'

'Yes, I will try. To begin with you are quite right. I was in that room while you and Mr. Newman were having your talk.'

She stopped as she saw my head moving from side to side. 'If you were in there, and you were, you heard what was said. Now if we're really going to get anywhere, we'll have to dispense with this Mr. Newman tag. You don't have to be coy with me, I'm supposed to be on your team.'

'Very well. I'm in love with Eddie Newman. Things were reaching a stage where I would have had to talk to my husband. Does that satisfy you?'

She looked me in the eyes. Her shoulders were straight and her head was up. I knew at that moment that the love Marcia Van Huizen had for Ed Newman was the right kind, leaving aside the moral issue that she'd been a married woman when it started. That was none of my business, and anyway it was no longer true.

'That'll do to get us started. How long

have you and Ed known each other?'

'Almost from the time he first came here. About three months ago.'

'How did you come to meet him?'

'What has all this got to do — ?'

'Uh uh,' I wagged my finger. 'Please take no notice of the questions. Mostly the answers won't tell me anything at all. And I'm certainly not prying into your private life. After all, you'll be getting married now, I guess. No harm in telling me, is there?'

'I suppose you're right. Yes, we'll be getting married. Not right away, with poor Ben just dead. In a couple of months probably.'

'Fine. Now, how did you first meet Ed Newman?'

'At the Club. It was a new place, everybody was going there.'

'Your husband took you?'

'Ben? No, I went with Dean Hillier. He's quite a gambler, you know. If ever I feel like having a evening of roulette or some other game, Dean always knows where to take me. He was playing tonight.'

'Uh huh. Is he a heavy player?'

'He used to bet very heavily. I believe he lost quite a lot of money to Mr. Kalmus. Ben warned him about it. He's paid what he owes, or so I understand.'

'I see.' I took the empty glass from her hand and went over to replenish it. If she screamed for me to stop, I didn't hear anything. 'Seems like a nice guy, Hillier.'

'Oh, he's all right. Better than some we've had,' she returned.

I handed over her drink.

'Your husband had trouble with his private secretaries?'

'Oh, no, not real trouble. But it's a strain, you know, carrying around all that confidential information in your head, and being available twenty-four hours a day.'

'How do you mean, twenty-four hours a day?' I asked.

'I'm exaggerating, of course. But the private secretary always has to live with us as well as being at the office all day. If Dean wants a few hours off, he can always have it, but Ben has to know — had to know — where he could contact him if necessary.'

I agreed that a job like that would soon get to be a strain.

'Surely you must have found it a nuisance sometimes, having an extra man around the house the whole time I mean.'

There was more to the question than the words said, and I could see by the quick flash of her eyes that she'd got the rest of it. She shrugged.

'With one or two of them there have been moments of — difficulty. Poor dears, after all I was the only woman they saw most of the time.'

'I don't know a man who would consider that a matter for deep mourning, if you don't mind my saying so.'

She inclined her head in a graceful little bow.

'Now you're going to ask me if I ever had trouble of that kind with Dean Hillier,' she announced.

'Did you?'

'He came to us about — oh — ten months or so ago. We both liked him. There were a couple of occasions early on when he made cow-eyes at me, but that was all. I gave him a very clear notion from the start of just what his duties were supposed to be.'

'I see. And nothing since then? What about him escorting you to the gaming joints?'

'Quite harmless. We both like to gamble, Ben doesn't.'

It was unnerving somehow, the way she referred to her dead husband half the time as though he were alive. Then she added,

'Anyway, Dean has a girl of his own.'

'That's interesting. Anyone I'm likely to know?'

'I'm really only guessing, I certainly don't know any name. But Ben used to go to San Francisco a lot on business. Dean always had an extra kind of liveness about him when one of the trips was due. I'm certain he has a girl there.'

'But he doesn't talk about her?'

'No. In fact, he got quite annoyed one day when I teased him about her. Said it was only because all women were incurably romantic and couldn't bear to think of a man being reasonably happy

215

without one. Just the same, I am convinced there is such a girl.'

I made a mental note to take an interest in Hillier's girl later. At the moment I was more concerned with things closer to home.

'I'd like to ask what you know about George Porter.'

'That's the man Eddie mentioned to you. He got to know about us somehow, and has been making Eddie give him money. He's been threatening to go to my husband.'

'It sounds like the kind of work Porter was good at,' I assented.

'You know him?'

Whenever she was surprised, I'd noticed that her nostrils had a habit of flaring slightly.

'Well, in a way. He was a no-good loafer, a guy who'd sell his own grandmother for a shot of bar whisky. When they swept him up off the street, they should have dumped him with the other garbage, instead of taking up space in the city morgue.'

'A long speech for you. And no

question on the end of it. What had Porter done to you, Mr. Preston?'

'To me, nothing. But a friend of mine, a senior police officer here in Monkton, had a very bad time for a few weeks, when Porter was caught with hush money sticking to his dirty fingers.'

'You mean he was a policeman?'

I'd been right about the nostrils.

'No, he was never a policeman. But he had a uniform and a badge, and he was on the City payroll. There'll be some happy cops in this town tomorrow when they find out he's dead.'

'I can't say the news caused me any deep feeling of personal loss either.'

'I can imagine. According to Ed Newman, Porter was on his way to see me when he was killed. Why would he do that? I mean with your husband dead he'd got nobody to sell to.'

She looked at me carefully before saying anything.

'Mr. Preston, I think you can be trusted. It wouldn't do if certain people had any inkling of what I'm going to tell you.'

When people say they're going to trust me, it makes me uneasy. Usually it's the prelude to being handed some piece of information that's as hot as a stove. That, or a pack of large lies.

'Before you tell me, let me say something. If you're going to give me some information the police ought to have, don't. Anything that even looks like concealment of incriminating evidence or compounding a felony, and you can trust me just as far as that telephone.'

'You're a curious man,' she said musingly. 'There's no suggestion of anything of the kind. Quite a different matter. You see, Mr. Preston, when a man like Benedict Van Huizen dies there are — repercussions. Financial repercussions.'

'You mean everybody on Wall Street sells everything connected with the combine?'

She nodded. The jet hair gleamed as the movement caught the light reflection.

'It's a temporary business, normally. People get nervous, particularly with a case of suicide. You can't blame them.

The market drops a few points until the affairs of the company concerned have been investigated, then everything goes back to normal.'

'If the company is still in the black,' I pointed out.

She laughed at that. I hadn't heard her laugh before. It was a joyful, bubbly sound, not altogether matching the clipped tones of her speaking voice. Evidently the finishing school hadn't been entirely successful in correcting her sense of humour.

'You must forgive me, but the very suggestion that the Van Huizen Corporation could be anything but a goldmine was really quite amusing.'

'I guess it does sound kind of silly. Please go on.'

'With Ben's death we had to expect something of the kind. There was some selling, and the stock in one or two subsidiary companies did drop a point or two. By next week that will all have been straightened out.'

I began to see which way she was heading. I don't have a head for the market myself. To me, the difference between a bull and a bear is a pair of horns. But I did know enough to realise that under certain conditions the affairs of even quite large corporations can be decided by a few unfavourable reports in the Press.

'You're going to say that after your husband's death, Porter changed his tactics. His new approach was that unless the goose kept up the supply of golden eggs, he'd spread your romance with Newman across the front page. You couldn't take the risk of what that might do to the combine, especially your share in it, that right?'

'Something on those lines.'

'With so much at stake, why didn't you just pay him off? You could have preferred charges once the business of the estate was cleared up.'

'Exactly what I said to Eddie. But he wouldn't hear of it. He can be very forceful, you know.'

I was prepared to go along with that.

'I know. I used to watch him sometimes a few years back. One of the guys he got forceful with had his jaw broken in three places.'

The dark brown eyes shone.

'You saw him fight? Oh, I would have loved that. He's shown me one or two newsreels of his fights, but it isn't quite the same, is it?'

Not quite the same, lady. I wondered whether Ed had shown her any newsreel shots of his tank jobs, the ones where he was doing the fancy diving act, while the lads in the tight overcoats and wide-brimmed fedoras were counting up the take. On balance, I thought he'd have overlooked those, and this was no time to bring them up.

'So Eddie wouldn't have any part of Porter's new deal. What reason did he have?'

'He said he wasn't going to be pushed around by a person like that. In any case, with Porter's reputation what it was in Monkton City, Ed said no newspaperman would believe him.'

'Well, you know your own business best, but I'd have said that was taking a long chance.'

'I thought so. When Eddie told this man what we'd decided, he said he knew somebody the papers would believe, somebody who'd be glad of a half-share.'

'Me?'

It was foolish, but I was irritable about it. I don't say anybody would rate me for a presidential nomination, but I like to think my standing is a little higher than a guy who would buy into a deal like that. Maybe it was a lie. Maybe Marcia Van Huizen or Ed Newman or both of them sent George Porter on the long journey to prevent him getting to me with his story and — . No, that wouldn't do either. They didn't have to kill him. All he wanted was money, and it would have been a lot less trouble just to give it to him. As I sat there thinking, Marcia put her own construction on what was going on in my head.

'If that annoyed you, I'm sorry.' She sounded as though she meant it.

'Oh no, no it didn't annoy me. You should hear some of the things I get called. Mrs. Van Huizen, how much money had George Porter taken from you up till now?'

'Just under a thousand dollars, I believe. I haven't dealt with him, luckily. Ed has seen to all that.'

'Not very much, is it? I mean, considering the status of the customer. I'd have thought a lot more than that.'

'It was his intention, so he told Ed, to take a modest five hundred dollars a week for the rest of his life. That way he wouldn't have to worry about an unexplainable large sum for the revenue people to query.'

George Porter had been smarter than I'd realised.

'Nice of him to think that one out. Five hundred a week is a lot of money. Could you meet it out of your own resources? I mean, leaving your husband's estate out of it for now.'

'I could, yes. I have ample private means.'

It seemed a little unfair that a girl with all the advantages Nature could bestow should also have an unlimited supply of the world's goods. It seemed to me that with either one, she didn't need the other. But maybe I was grouchy. Maybe it was five o'clock in the morning and I was tired. And somewhere a little voice was muttering something about maybe I couldn't see why it should be Ed Newman and not Mark Preston.

'Whatever Porter had on his mind, we don't have to worry about him any more.' I thought I'd change the subject. 'I'd like to tell you something. Something I think you have a right to know.'

She'd been sitting back in the chair while Porter was on the menu. Now she leaned forward, suddenly interested again.

'I think you were quite right the first time I met you. I think your husband was murdered.' I went on with the story, what there was of it.

I told her about the County Sheriff and the insurance company; about the straight cop named Harrigan and the other kind, Dunphy. I told her other things, some facts, a lot of guesses. She listened in that steel-spring attitude, nodding occasionally, asking a question. Marcia was a smart girl, you didn't need to draw any pictures. Just tell her once and she had it. When I was through she said,

'You've been very busy, Mr. Preston. And mostly on my behalf. I'm grateful.'

It sounded as though she meant it.

'It's not finished yet,' I reminded her. 'Next we have to find out who killed your husband, don't we?'

'Of course. Why do you say it like that?'

I wound up for the curved ball. It was one of those times I hate the business I'm in.

'Has it occurred to you what the police would make of this, supposing they knew what I know?'

'Go on.' The words were almost inaudible.

'Here we have a murder, made to look like a suicide. Maybe somebody did give the killer a little help, after the fact as they say, but that's become unimportant to the main enquiry. So we start clean. Big industrialist murdered. Why? No financial difficulties, no business problems, not the kind to cause a murder anyhow. Domestic situation, not so good. Wife in love with ex-fighter turned gambler's assistant.'

Some of the restlessness had returned to Marcia Van Huizen. She fiddled with the platinum strap of her tiny watch.

'You're talking nonsense, of course.'

'No, I'm not,' I told her quietly. 'I'm talking plain horse sense. Why, there isn't a copper in the business who wouldn't jump at a set-up like this.'

She got up from the chair and walked across to where I'd left her coat.

'You're annoying me, Mr. Preston. I don't intend to remain here and let you do it.'

I followed her quickly to the door and held it shut.

'Stand aside,' she ordered. There was a dark flush of anger in her cheeks stretching down into the slim throat.

I stood to one side. She grasped the handle again and pulled the door open.

'If you leave now, I shall have to assume you've something to hide,' I said gently.

For a moment she stood quite still, undecided. Then, very slowly, she released her grip on the handle. With one foot I clicked the door. She stood there, looking as miserable a girl as I've seen.

'It won't be long before the police come to see me again, will it?' The voice sounded forlorn.

'My guess is that you've got to face this tomorrow. And you won't be able to walk out on those guys.'

The brown shoulders shrugged and the corners of her deep red lips turned down.

'What do you want to know?'

'Where were you on Tuesday night?'

'At the Club Rendezvous, I was there with Eddie.'

'The whole night?'

'No. There was a large party of moving picture people coming to gamble. They were only going to play for a few hours, then go on to some house party. Dean had arranged it as a favour to Mr. Kalmus. I didn't want to stay while they were there, so I went out for a while.'

'And went back to the Club afterwards?'

She nodded.

'Oh, yes, Eddie and I were able to — er

— talk for a half-hour or so. Then I went home.'

I pushed another cigarette into my face. When I held out the pack she waved it away.

'What time was all this?'

'I don't know exactly. I didn't take any especial notice.' She thought about it. 'Let's see, it would have been some time after nine when I left and I went back before midnight.'

'Where'd you go?'

'To the open-air movie at Palamino. Does it matter?'

'It begins to. The Club Rendezvous is a little less than an hour's ride from your home. Your husband was murdered at ten-thirty. Do you think it matters where you were?'

Her face changed from a look of dejection to something else. Something that might have been worry.

'But the theatre, somebody will remember me.'

As patiently as possible I crossed that one off.

'Mrs. Van Huizen, nobody is going to

remember you. Everybody was in cars the same as you were. It was night-time. Even the people who really went to see the movie are not going to be able to identify you positively.'

'But the stub, surely if I can find that — '

'No, it won't do either. What does it prove? You went in. Nobody's going to stand up and swear you didn't turn right around and come out again.'

She nodded dully.

'I think you're right. The programme won't help me either, will it? Because if I had to know what the picture was about, I could have gone before or since and seen it.'

I felt uncomfortable. Every instinct told me to comfort this girl. Everything is going to be all right. But was it? No matter what I privately thought or felt, the fact remained that Marcia Van Huizen was up there with the front runners when it came to opportunity to kill her husband. And I've been taken on the roundabouts by too many good-looking women to deceive myself that she couldn't possibly have done it. She possibly could, and nobody had a better motive.

'I'd be lying if I said I don't think you're in a spot.' It was as gentle as I could make it.

She nodded miserably, then laughed without humour.

'I'm afraid the situation finds me without experience to call on. What do I do now, transfer all my securities to a South American republic and get on the next plane out?'

'I wouldn't recommend it. Go home and go to bed. I'll do what I can. There's plenty about all this we don't know yet. I'll just nose around and see what I can find.'

Impulsively she laid a hand on my arm.

'Somehow I don't like to mention money to you, but what I said the other night stands. Find out who killed my husband, Mr. Preston, and you won't regret it.'

'That's what I had in mind,' I told her. 'By the way, I suppose Hillier will have moved out now that — now that you're alone in the house.'

'Yes. He booked a room in some hotel yesterday. The Apache, I think. Did you want to see him?'

'Nothing special. Just wanted to know where everybody was.'

After that there wasn't much to talk about. She stayed another two or three minutes, then left. I phoned Joe and told him to take a walk, followed her downstairs just to be sure Joe did as I asked. He was nowhere in sight as I watched Marcia climb into the low green coupé and drive off.

Upstairs I checked my watch. It was a few minutes before six a.m. I cursed the time, which moved too fast to suit me. The bed looked great. I poked the soft mattress with my forefinger and felt the springy resilience. Then I went and put on some coffee. No bed for old Sherlock Preston this night, or morning I should say. I had a very light meal of coffee and benzedrine tablets, then crawled under a shower. This is supposed to be a refreshing thing to do. I guess it worked at that. Before the shower I could have slept for a month, afterwards ten days would have been plenty enough. When I telephoned Ed Newman, he didn't sound pleased.

'What in hell is the idea? Do you know what time it is? Have you lost your marbles?'

It made me feel better. I didn't see why I should be the only one to be inconvenienced.

'Woke you up, huh?' I said it without sympathy.

'What else? I just got to bed an hour ago.'

'Well, I'm real sorry, Ed. Want to see you right away.'

'It'll keep. Right now I'm going back to sleep.'

Before he could bang down the receiver, I said quickly, 'No, Ed, no you're not. I'll be over in twenty minutes. Let's talk about murder.' Then I put down the phone.

I was pretty confident that the exit line would guarantee an awake Newman when I got to the Club.

8

The side door, which I knew led to the two upstairs apartments, was unlocked. The cold early daylight made the *décor* of the Club look shabby and cheap as I climbed the stairs. I felt the .38 rubbing against my left side as I went up, and the discomfort was one I was very pleased to suffer. The narrow passage at the top was in darkness and I flicked down a switch on the wall. Frank Kalmus evidently believed in comfort judging by the new deep pile carpet in the passage-way. I found myself with a choice of two doors, one on each side. After a little listening, I thought there were faint sounds behind one of them. I tapped softly.

'It's open,' growled a voice. Newman's.

I opened it carefully and looked inside. There was a lot of expensive white-painted furniture on view. The heavy gold silk curtains were drawn across and in front of them was a deep-lounging divan covered in the same material. In the middle of the divan was the man I'd come to see. He looked at me sourly.

'Well?'

I was glad he hadn't jumped me the second I got inside the door. For one thing, it would have complicated the visit, and for another, I wasn't forgetting the guy was an ex-contender. Not that he looked very impressive at that moment. He was beginning to show a blue shave, and the red quilted dressing-gown was pulled all round him anyhow, not like the man in the advertisements.

'O.K. to sit down?' I queried.

He shrugged and took a deep drag on his cigarette. The atmosphere in the place was thick enough, an open window would have been a good idea. I hadn't seen Newman with his guard down before. All the dames and what-have-you had left more signs on his face than I'd realised. Still I only ever saw the guy under artificial light, and that is by no means the same thing as a shaft of early morning sun.

'Preston, you get in my hair. I told you

a few hours back where we stand. This new joke better be very funny.'

I sat down in a high-backed chair that had no arms. It was as far away from him as I could get and would allow a little time for me to move if he exploded.

'You're gonna be disappointed, Ed. This isn't funny at all.'

He ground out the cigarette in a silver tray, took another from the box on the table and held a flame from a heavy embossed silver lighter. It was a long trip from the all-comers booths in the steel towns, and Ed Newman was evidently no believer in the spartan life. When the butt was drawing, he said through a cloud of smoke,

'Something about a murder, wasn't it?'

'Something,' I agreed.

'You talked to Marcia, I guess. She left right after you.'

'I been talking to a lot of people. Most of 'em you don't even know. Still, as you mention her first, let's talk about Marcia.'

He got up from the divan, changed his mind, sat down again. I was relieved.

'So what about her? I told you where we stand when you were here before.' He looked at me. There was no friendliness in the look. 'You figured out an angle for blackmail after all? That what you're doing here?'

'Be your age, Newman. If I was going to blackmail two people, I'd go to the one with the dough. That would about let you out, wouldn't it?'

I'd wondered whether that would be enough to bring him after me, but I'd reckoned without his ring training. In that game you don't lose your temper early in the bout or you're a dead duck. Newman breathed heavily and his large right hand clenched and unclenched, but he stayed in his corner.

'I'll remember you said that. Naturally a guy like you has to figure a percentage. It wouldn't enter your cesspit of a mind that I might love the girl, would it?'

I smiled cheerfully.

'What gives between you and Marcia Van Huizen is no concern of mine. I'm looking for a killer. Marcia is paying me to look. If it turns out to be you — or

236

Marcia for that matter — it won't make any difference.'

'But you still take her money, huh? I ought to break both your arms and heave you out the window.'

It was still only talk. He hadn't moved from where he was sitting. I unbuttoned my jacket as though it was too hot in the room. That would save one second's delay if I had to bring up the artillery. Then I said,

'About what you told me a couple of hours ago. It needs a re-write.'

'Huh?' He was puzzled.

'All that crap about love's young dream and how you and Marcia would face the world together with celestial choir and full orchestral backing.'

Newman said in a measured tone,

'Just what does that mean?'

'It means you were grandstanding, Ed. Marcia was right there in the room with us.'

'She told you that?'

'She didn't need to. I hate to brag, but it's my business to work out these little things.'

'So she was there. If what I said wasn't true, she'd have heard me, ain't that so?'

Very slowly I moved my head negatively from side to side.

'No. That ain't necessarily so, as the saying goes. What Marcia heard she thought was the truth. There's a difference.'

'Go ahead. Tell me about the difference.'

He had moved his weight a little and was now in a position to flex his toes and be on his feet in no seconds flat.

'George Porter was on his way to see me when he died. He was going to tell me something, maybe a lot of things.'

'And?'

'And one of those things was the reason he was blackmailing you. You, Ed. Not you and Marcia.'

If he jumped now I'd have maybe two seconds in which to stand clear and get the .38 in a position where it would be of some use.

'Go ahead, little man. What have you got in that peanut brain?'

I liked him better when he growled.

This soft-spoken routine was a Newman I didn't know.

'Porter was on to something you couldn't have Marcia knowing. It was cool of you to pitch her that tale of yours and let her use her own money to prevent her finding it out.'

'I had to. Don't you see, I — '

He stopped almost as soon as he started.

'Go on, Ed, what don't I see?'

'No.' He shook his head impatiently. 'This is your tale. You pitch it. How do I know you got anything at all?'

'All right, then here it is. You're an ex-fighter. Before you came here you lived in San Francisco. In that town the fight crowd hangs around a hash joint run by one Tinplate Terence O'Neil. There was a girl worked there, a redhead. Her name was Cheryl Morley.'

When I spoke the name, the line of his mouth went a little tighter, otherwise he was still.

'Cheryl was a good kid, but her brother kept her under wraps too much. She got herself mixed up with a guy, a guy with money and a name. Next thing she knows this guy up-anchors and leaves town. Before she's through crying about that, she finds out something else. She's going to have his child.'

Newman fidgeted around. So did I.

'I don't know what she did next. Probably wrote him and got no answer. In the end she blew town herself and headed for the man she was certain would help her. She used a new name, rented an apartment and got in touch with this guy. But she was out of luck. In the three months since coming to Monkton City the hero of the story has got another girl. A beauty, and with a bankroll. The guy says he's hung on the new dame and that's maybe true for all I know, but it doesn't help Cheryl much.'

Suddenly Newman dropped his head in between his hands and sobbed.

'If only she'd waited I'd have fixed the kid up.'

'Would you, Ed? Did you tell her that?'

'No. No, you see she wasn't normal. It had made her kind of funny somehow.'

'It's liable to. All you had to do was put

the phone down and forget it. She couldn't do that. What happened?'

He was in control of himself again.

'What makes this any of your business, anyhow?'

'That has to be a joke. Sure it's my business. Cheryl Morley, or Vickers as she called herself, was pregnant. You were responsible and George Porter found that out. Now Cheryl's dead, Porter's dead and you're all set to marry millions. You ask me what makes it my business; that has to be a joke.'

'All right, Preston, so you're a smart guy. Laugh at this one.'

From the dressing-gown he produced a large automatic and pointed it at me. Suddenly the room was very still. I could see by his face that Newman meant business with the gun. My voice was shaky.

'That's not a very good idea, Ed.'

'No? This is a place of business, there's plenty money lying around. So I woke up one morning and there's a guy prowling around outside. I stick this on him,' tapping the gun, 'but he jumps me just the same. Next thing I know there's a bang. The guy is dead. The law won't like it, but they'll buy.'

'Maybe. And even if they do, Marcia won't stand for it. You aren't gonna hit any jackpot with that thing, even if you hit me. What's got into you, anyhow?'

'I'm about sick and tired of questions. Questions from you, Marcia, everybody. This whole thing is around my neck. So maybe I knew Cheryl one time, maybe it was my kid, I don't know. Porter soon tied her to me, and held his hand out right off. That's true. I didn't kill either one of 'em and that's true too, but there ain't a jury in the country would go for it. Now you've worked out the deal all by yourself, but it won't be any help where you're going.' His knuckles tightened around the trigger.

I shouted,

'For Pete's sake, Ed — '

But I never got it finished. The heavy automatic roared and I flung myself to the floor, chair as well. The slug tore into the wall behind where I'd been sitting. I had the .38 in my hand as Newman jumped up and moved his body to get a second try. It was no time for arguing. I rolled hard across the carpet, banging my shoulder painfully against a heavy wooden cabinet. Newman's face was working with rage as the .38 swung towards me. The gun in my hand kicked, and the roar was enough to wake the dead. Without waiting to see what had happened, I threw myself behind the cabinet and edged my head round the other side. The war was over. Newman was standing quite still in the middle of the room, right hand pressed over the dressing-gown. A couple of large splashes had reached the pale grey carpet where they lay sticky beside the dropped automatic. I put the iron back under my shoulder and stepped out, kicking Newman's gun to the far side of the room. He looked at me emptily, pain suddenly filling his face.

'Am I gonna die, Preston?' The voice was wheezy, the words squeezed out by an effort.

'Could be. Anything you wanta tell me, Ed?'

Suddenly he staggered. It was amazing he hadn't keeled over before this. I tried to catch him, but was still inches short when he dropped like a sack of potatoes. I bent over him. A voice snapped,

'Freeze right there or I'll blow off your head.'

Cautiously I looked over my shoulder. Frank Kalmus stood framed in the doorway. In his pudgy hand was a forty-five calibre service revolver that really would blow my head off. When he saw who I was, he looked worried.

'Preston? This your play?'

'No time for talk, Kalmus. This guy needs a doctor and damned quick.'

'We'll talk first. This anything to do with my business?'

'No. Outside stuff. It ties in with three murders, and if you want to make it four, this is the time. I'm getting a doctor.'

I got up off the floor and headed for the gold-coloured telephone. I got emergency and told my tale fast. Kalmus didn't do anything to stop me, but kept the revolver pointed in my direction. When I was through I turned back to him.

'At this time of the morning those guys will be here in five minutes. If you're going to blow any heads off, you better get busy.'

'Ah,' he said disgustedly. Then he poked the heater into the side pocket of the coat he'd thrown over his pyjamas. 'I'm no gunman, anyhow. Strictly a gambler.'

He walked over to Newman and stood looking down at him. The colour was gone from the face of the man on the floor and his breathing was short and rapid.

'This is bad about Ed. You wanta tell me about it?'

I found some liquor in a cupboard, poured myself a jolt and tipped it down. It was noticeable that the hand holding the glass was shaking like the last leaf on a tall tree in a high wind. When I didn't answer him, Kalmus said thoughtfully,

'Have it your way. The law boys'll take care of you, I guess. Just like to say something, though. I don't go for rough stuff. Hoods and such, they're out of my line. But you get this, Preston, and you get it good. Ed was one of my boys, and I look after my boys. If you ain't got a good yarn to cover this, the town is going to get unhealthy.'

'You're a mile wide, Kalmus. Ed was playing his own game, as well as yours. This has got nothing to do with your business at all.'

The Scotch wasn't doing anything for me. I felt slightly sick. I kept looking at Newman lying on the floor. He looked like hell to me, and his breathing was very faint. If he died, it was me killed him. He had a gun and he'd tried to kill me, but I was lucky and it was pure chance that I wasn't spilling my life blood on that carpet. Only I wasn't. Newman was, and I put him there. Not that the law was worrying me. Those boys would soon piece it together and there'd be no complaint sheet against Mark Preston for this little mix-up. I'd be as free as a bird. Only I had to lie in bed nights trying to sleep, trying to tell myself there was nothing else I could do. It wouldn't make any difference. Newman's face would hang there half-way between the bed and the ceiling, and sleep would be a stranger for many a long empty night. I knew all about it, it had happened to me before. At the thought, I shuddered and clattered some more liquor into the glass. Kalmus was still in the room.

'Seems to me a guy who goes around killing people ought to get used to it.'

'Shut up, damn you, Kalmus.'

He laughed softly. I remembered that I wanted to talk to this man. Now seemed as good a time as any.

'How about some free information?' I asked.

'You got plenty of nerve, after this.' He waved the .45 towards Ed.

'So I got plenty of nerve. How much did Hillier owe you?'

'Ask him.'

'I'm asking you. If you tell me I'll do you a favour.'

'Like what?'

'Like not telling the law what the boys in your back room are doing every night.'

His face darkened and the hand holding the gun tightened.

247

'You're a sweet guy, Preston. It was fourteen grand.'

I whistled.

'Good round sum. When did he pay you?'

'Last week-end. Gimme a cheque.'

'I hope for your sake you've already cleared it.'

He didn't have time to make a reply because there was a commotion outside and two guys in white coats and a young medico bustled in. They spotted Newman and went to him. Then came a fat middle-aged guy in a blue flannel suit. Him I didn't know. He looked at me, then Kalmus, then took in everything in the room. Last, but by no means least, came Detective Schultz of the Homicide Squad.

'You're off limits, Schultzie,' I greeted him. 'The guy's not dead yet.'

Schultz looked at me sourly. Already his young face was getting furrowed over with habitual lines of suspicion.

'The desk sergeant who got the report from the hospital spotted your name and knew I'd be interested. You want to do it here or down at headquarters?'

'Headquarters for me,' I replied.

'O.K., let's go.' He turned to Blue-suit. 'Vince, get pictures of everything in sight, will you? Don't forget that,' he pointed to the hole in the wall made by Newman's shot. Schultz didn't miss a trick. 'I'll have two of the boys come and give you a hand. Mister, are you coming like that or do you want to get some clothes on?'

Kalmus started.

'Me? But I'm not mixed up in this. It was all over when I got here,' he protested.

'You're in it now. Go get dressed,' was the terse reply.

'Lay off him, Schultzie. That's Frank Kalmus, he owns the joint. He only came over to see what all the noise was about.'

Schultz stared at me with a stony face. Then he rubbed the side of his nose with a thick forefinger.

'That's on the level?' When I nodded, he turned back to the gambler. 'We'll get to you later. Don't leave the building. One of the men who comes down here can get your statement.'

'Right.'

Kalmus was clearly uncertain as to whether or not he ought to thank me. In the end he decided against it. The two attendants had got Newman onto a stretcher now. Schultz looked enquiringly at the doctor, a youngster not much older than himself.

'Well, Doc?'

The doctor looked from one to the other of us. I thought privately it was most likely his first ride. He laughed importantly.

'It's hard to say, officer. The man has lost a good deal of blood. No vital organs seem to have been damaged, however, and I would say our patient was a very husky specimen. He may have a chance, but I won't commit myself at this stage.'

Schultz nodded.

'Well, Preston, we may have to struggle along with attempted murder. Still, in your case even that's better than nothing.'

I wasn't in the mood for Schultz.

'Here,' I dived under my arm and pulled out the .38. The doctor and the one called Vince took an alarmed step backwards. I held the iron out to Schultz. 'The lethal weapon. Exhibit A. You know the rules, Schultzie. When locking up the killer, always remove all machine-guns, sawn-offs and other offensive weapons.'

He flushed slightly and shoved the .38 into a pocket.

'All right, snap it up, Preston. Let's get outa here.'

Even at that time in the a.m. there were twenty or more rubbernecks in the car park, pointing to the ambulance and the police sedan. When we hit the veranda, they swung around to get a gander at us. Schultz hadn't bothered to put the arm on me. Quickly I grabbed him round the elbow, walking slightly behind him. The crowd muttered and nudged each other. Schultz hadn't latched on to what was happening, but so far as the innocent by-standers were concerned, he was elected. One or two remarks drifted towards us and suddenly the young detective grew very red round the neck. Angrily he turned to me.

'What's the gag, Preston? Get the hand off my arm.'

He tried to jerk free, but I held on tight.

'Take it easy, killer. We know how to deal with your kind at headquarters,' I snapped.

There were approving murmurs from our little audience. We were almost up to the car now. Schultz was stuttering with rage.

'I'll murder you, Preston. I'll smear you all over the walls when we get down to the station.'

The looks on the faces of one or two of the spectators signified that he'd better not try it.

'You O.K., officer?' This from a very large character in dungarees.

'O.K. thanks, buddy.' I smiled at him. Then to Schultz, 'You drive. I need both hands to watch you.'

He climbed in behind the wheel, his face working with suppressed fury. I walked around front and got in the other door. The big guy leaned in.

'I'll ride as far as the station if you want. This guy has a mean-looking face.'

'I can handle him, thanks just the same.'

Schultz started her up, almost jerking my helper off his feet. Then we moved away. Nothing was said during the ten-minute ride. I was busy with my own thoughts and didn't want to get involved in a slanging match with Schultz. He pulled up at the kerb outside the front entrance to Police Headquarters. I got out of the heap and walked around to the sidewalk. Together we entered the building and climbed the steep flights of stairs to the third floor. My escort was calmer now, but there was a granite set to his face that boded no good for somebody. Somebody who would turn out to be me. He opened the door and motioned me to lead the way inside. I didn't mind because Schultz was not the kind of cop a man thought twice before turning his back on. Gil Randall was in the room, sitting on a cane chair which was tilted at a dangerous angle against the wall.

'So Schultzie finally caught up with you, uh, Preston?'

'Yeah, in a way. All I had to do with it

was call and tell him where I was and what had happened. Trapped in the act of escaping, you might say.'

Schultz said nothing.

'Better let us have the story, Mark. Or what passes for a story in the present instance,' said Randall. The cane chair creaked ominously.

'Seems I had a misunderstanding with Ed Newman,' I told him.

'It also seems Ed is over at the City General bleeding like a stuck pig. There has to be more story.'

Randall waved his hand at me languidly, like a traffic cop at a busy intersection on a hot day.

'I'll start at the beginning. Newman has been making time with Mrs. Van Huizen for the past three months. Suddenly Mr. Van Huizen commits suicide, which is very considerate of him from where Ed is sitting. Being an obliging sort of fellow, Mr. Van Huizen goes out to kill a girl first, a girl named Cheryl Vickers.'

'Why would that be obliging? I get the bit about what a handy time it was for the husband to blow his brains out. But the girl, where does she figure in Ed's life?'

Anybody who didn't know Randall would have thought he was half asleep.

'Cheryl Vickers was pregnant. Ed Newman was responsible.'

'You say. So why was she putting the bite on Van Huizen, and why did he kill himself?' Randall shook his head slowly. 'This don't feel right.'

'You're behind with your information, Gil. Five'll get you ten Van Huizen was murdered.'

'Mark, Mark,' he was trying to be patient. 'It's all on the file. The County Sheriff's office — '

' — Is run by a crooked political appointee. Not by a cop,' I finished for him.

'Oh, no.' It was the first thing Schultz had said. 'Now we're going to get the crooked administration bit.'

'That's right, Schultzie.'

The phone rang. Schultz glowered at me, picked the instrument up and screwed it against his ear.

'Yeah? Yeah, he's here,' he looked up at me. 'O.K., Lieutenant. Yeah, I'll tell him.'

He put down the receiver and spoke to Randall. 'That was Rourke. Says he's having breakfast over at Big Fritz's. Wants this guy to get over there right away.'

Randall nodded.

'We'll nail this one down later, Mark. You heard what he said.'

I went to where Schultz sat and held out my hand.

'The .38,' I told him. 'It's in your pocket.'

'This a gag? You just got through shooting one guy with it.'

'That's right, I did. You charging me with anything?'

'I don't know yet. We haven't heard the tale — '

'You gonna keep me here for anything?'

'Hell, no. You heard me say Rourke wanted you.' Schultz was uncomfortable.

'Then you've no reason to hold my gun. I have a licence for it. You want me to call a cop, and charge you as a larcenous public servant?'

Randall tittered and his chair scraped against the wall. As though he were sawing off his leg, Schultz placed the automatic slowly on the table.

'Thanks. If I knock off anybody else, I'll ring you and tell you where to find me.'

I got out before Schultz lost his temper. Big Fritz's was a feed-bag run by an ex-patrolman, and popular with people from the Department. It was only a few blocks and as I stepped along in the bright sunshine, I wondered why Rourke was having his breakfast there. He hadn't been due for night duty and Mrs. Rourke was a great hand with the skillet. I found him sitting in a corner booth stuffing into a vast heap of scrambled eggs. There was a pile of toast on the side and a coffee cup that was seeing plenty of action, too. John waved to me when I went in, but didn't hold up his work. I noticed one very unusual thing about the man. He hadn't shaved.

'Sit down, Mark. We can talk while I eat.'

I slid into the opposite bench. The eggs looked good. A large blonde came and stood beside me. She was Hannah, one of Fritz's three daughters, and one of the three reasons the place was so popular with young law-men.

' 'Lo, Hannah. I'll take the same, but ease off on the portions.'

She showed me her nice white teeth and went off to set up the food. I said,

'What gives, John? What's so important it can't wait till you finish your breakfast?'

'Owe you something, Mark. Harrigan dragged me out of bed at five o'clock this morning. I ought to hate you for that, but I don't. Know why?'

'No.'

'Harrigan got all hipped up last night. Account of something you told him. Does it begin to click?'

'Not very loud. I told Harrigan about a little guessing I'd been doing. He was going to take another look at it this morning.'

Another large forkful of egg disappeared down Rourke's throat. I wished Hannah would rush it up with my order. An empty fork waved at me.

'Couldn't wait. Harrigan, I mean. Thought it over after he left you. Got so hopping mad, he went to see Dunphy.'

'In the middle of the night?'

Rourke chuckled across the coffee cup, winced as the scalding liquid touched his lips.

'You don't know Harrigan. That guy is all cop. He dragged Dunphy out of the sack and — er — questioned him. Dunphy talked it up so fast Harrigan could hardly keep track.'

'So he did rig the room, huh?'

'Yup. When he got to the Van Huizen place, first thing he did was call his boss, the respected Sheriff of that County.'

'Who told him he was investigating a suicide unless Van Huizen's body had been sawn up and scattered round the room?'

'Right. Something like that, anyhow. Dunphy now says the window was open. There was a cigarette butt with lipstick on it, a monogrammed butt.'

'Could he read the monogram?' I was beginning to wish I hadn't come.

'It was a special kind that Marcia Van Huizen has made up for her. That wasn't all. He found a scarf inside the window.

One of those wispy bits of material the girls wear in the evening. She wouldn't notice whether it was on or off. Dunphy admits washing out the glass, too, just in case there was anything in it that shouldn't be.'

'I see. About the scarf, any more on that?'

'Sure. That was Marcia's too, no question about it.'

'How do you know? Have you seen it?'

Rourke shook his head happily.

'No. Dunphy found a buyer for it. Ed Newman paid him a thousand bucks for that scarf and the butt.'

I should have felt glad, but instead there was an empty feeling inside me. All right, so I wanted to prove a murder, and earn the money Benedict Van Huizen had paid me. But this I didn't want at all. Didn't even want to hear it.

'What's up, Mark? You don't look very pleased. After all, you get plenty of the credit for this, you know.'

'Great. You probably know about the fracas I had with Newman an hour ago?'

'Sure. One of the boys told me when I

came in here. That's how I knew where to find you.'

While he was talking, Hannah arrived with a heavy tray and started laying stuff in front of me. I thanked her and she told me to be sure and leave empty plates. I toyed around with the eggs, but it was no good. Suddenly I wasn't hungry any more. Rourke scrunched noisily at the last of the toast.

'Say, you must have been doing some fancy thinking, Mark. What put you on to Newman?'

'I wasn't on to the guy at all,' I replied.

'How was that?' He laughed. 'Ah, come on, shamus. You can tell an old friend. Or was it that you just felt like a shooting match with somebody and Ed Newman was the obvious choice?'

I wasn't feeling in the mood for too much of Rourke's humour.

'I went to the Club Rendezvous to straighten out a few things, that's all. Newman was kinda jumpy right off. Next thing I knew he threw down on me with this cannon, and then it was every man for himself.'

261

Rourke nodded sagely.

'Seen it a hundred times. There's a certain kind of man, when you get too close to him he snaps. You may not even have his name on your list, but he knows he's done it, whatever it is. You ask a couple of innocent questions and in his mind he's looking for the traps. Then he blows his top and it's all over. Why, just two months ago there was this jewellery store knocked over down on Seventeenth Avenue. They chilled the cashier. Randall and me went to see — '

He rambled on with the tale. I wasn't really listening. I was thinking about the City General Hospital and a man named Ed Newman who now had an extra hole in him. Courtesy of me. I was thinking about a woman who trusted me and who was now home in bed, while I sat at breakfast with a man who was about to go and arrest her. Rourke came to the end of his story and I made some suitable remarks. Then I said.

'Harrigan and you both figure Marcia Van Huizen for this deal?'

'What else? Here she's all tied in with

this Newman. Husband not the kind to give her a divorce. Put a girl with guts in a spot like that, something's gotta give.'

'Does she figure in his will, do you know?'

His brow puckered as he sorted through the mass of information inside his head.

'Yeah. We checked that as pure routine. Principal beneficiary. Plenty involved, too. Still, if we can hang this one on her, she won't draw a nickel. Against the law in this State for a murderer to profit by his victim's death.'

I signalled for more coffee. Hannah frowned at the untouched food, but said nothing.

'You putting the arm on Marcia?' I asked.

'Yup. Headquarters are hunting up a warrant right now. I'm going over there to pick it up in a few minutes.'

'Headquarters? You're pinching her for your killing, the Cheryl Vickers' thing?'

Rourke was busy lighting one of those evil black cheroots of his. Between puffs he wagged his head up and down.

'That's it. Harrigan was nervous about what might happen his end. If we moved on the County charge, no telling what strings might get pulled by a certain sheriff. We got a double killing here. Even in Monkton a smart counsellor might get away with a plea of extreme provocation. At the County they'd probably only charge her with culpable homicide and fine her fifty bucks or something screwy like that.'

'You mean her husband being the father of the Vickers girl's kid?'

'Sure. I can't see a jury handing out a first-degree verdict on this kind of set-up.'

I thought that over. There was nothing wrong with Rourke's reasoning. Where he was wrong was on his facts. I cursed quietly that I had said anything at all to Randall and Schultz. For the tenth part of a second I toyed with the idea of saying nothing to Rourke about Newman and Cheryl. Maybe Randall hadn't taken me very seriously. Maybe they wouldn't remember what I'd said. And maybe pigs have wings. If Rourke had called his office five minutes earlier — . But he hadn't, and all I could do now was to take away any chance Marcia Van Huizen might have had of a plea on a lesser count.

'I'm going to tell you something, John. I don't like telling you, but I already had it over with Gil and Schultz. You ought to be able to prosecute for first degree murder even now.'

'Huh? What's the big secret?'

'No secret any more, as the song goes. I think you could prove Ed Newman was the father of that child, not Van Huizen.'

He looked at me suspiciously through a haze of yellow smoke.

'What is this? I thought the Van Huizen woman was a client of yours?'

'That's right. But I forgot my manners this morning. I shoved a slug into a man. The police get nosey when that kind of thing happens. I already told Randall what I'm telling you now. Newman more or less admitted that he was responsible for Cheryl being the way she was. It was soon after that we started shooting.'

Rourke smacked his beefy fist against his leg.

'Terrific. Mark, now we got it sewn up

tight. A jealous woman kills her sweet-heart's pregnant girl-friend, then her own husband. What a difference to wronged wife. Why, the jury won't even recess for a verdict. The whole trial won't take two hours.'

'You'll excuse me if I'm not as excited as you,' I remarked sourly.

'Sure, Mark, sure. I know how you feel. Letting down your client, that's how you see it right now. But the law's the law. You're bound to get a guilty client now and then.'

That was true enough, but it didn't help me feel any better. The big policeman got up and tossed a bill and some small change on the table.

'That warrant should be about ready for me. You wanta come along on this pinch? Feel we owe you something on this.'

'No thanks, John. Isn't Harrigan going with you?'

'Meeting him near the house. Can't make an arrest on County territory without an accompanying officer from the Sheriff's office. You must know the rules by this time.'

'Of course. Well, I guess you'll be needing statements from me by the hundred. When do you want to start?'

'No hurry. Make it tonight, huh? I'll be busy all morning on this, and I got plenty of routine to catch up on this afternoon. Seven-thirty?'

'I'll be there.'

I waited till he was clear of the place before leaving myself. On the sidewalk three or four guys were talking.

'Say, here he is now.'

'Look this way, Preston.' Two bright flashes blotted out the sun for a second.

'How about a statement, Preston?'

'Is it true you and Newman fell out over a wealthy heiress?'

I brushed them away and walked off.

'Hey, give us a break, feller.'

They made a few remarks which didn't promise me too good a report in the midday editions. I waved to a crawling cab and hopped in. A few minutes later he dropped me off outside the Parkside Towers. Frank, the day man, seemed surprised to see me.

'Say, Mr. Preston, there was a bunch of

newspaper guys here asking for you.'

'I've seen 'em, Frank, thanks. Look, my car is in the forecourt of the Club Rendezvous. Have somebody get over there and pick it up right away, will you?'

I dropped the keys and a five-spot on the table.

'Sure thing, Mr. Preston. Right away. I'll go myself.'

Upstairs I put in a call to the Van Huizen house, but couldn't raise a reply. Then I tried to get hold of my San Francisco client, Rona Parsons, but didn't have any luck there either. After that I sat around smoking and thinking. A call to the City General produced the illuminating information that Mr. Newman was as well as could be expected, and if I wanted further particulars, I would have to talk to the police officer who was on duty at Mr. Newman's room. After about thirty minutes, that seemed more like thirty hours, Frank buzzed me to say he was back with the car.

9

The Apache Hotel is just short of the top-tax bracket. It's quiet and comfortable and plenty expensive, but somehow just misses being the place in town where the big money puts up its feet. The air was faintly perfumed as I walked into the lobby. It would never do for people paying these prices to have their sensitive nostrils offended by the disinfectant the cleaning staff had been using while said nostrils were resting on their lily-white pillows. It was nine-fifteen on a fine Thursday morning and I was going to have a little talk with one Dean Willman Hillier. A talk about murders galore, and a cheque made out to me in the sum of five hundred dollars. The guy behind the desk was a lulu. Black coat and vest, striped pants, and carnation glued to his lapel. His pale hands fluttered nervously above the gleaming counter.

'Good morning, sir.'

The voice was a confidential whisper, a you-and-I-are-the-only-ones-who-know kind of voice.

'I'd like to see Mr. Dean Hillier,' I whispered right back at him.

He picked up the peach telephone that was stationed by his hand.

'If you will kindly wait one moment, sir, I'll see if Mr. Hillier can receive you.'

I reached over and laid my fingers gently on his arm. He looked down in surprise not unmixed with distaste.

'Do you mind?' I smiled engagingly, I hoped. 'It's a kind of a surprise.'

I took my fingers away. The ten-dollar bill was folded neatly across his sleeve. He fingered it absently.

'It's most unusual, but Mr. Hillier is having a lot of visitors this morning. Tell me, sir, is it the gentleman's birthday, perhaps? I know the management would wish to express — '

'That's it,' I cut in. 'It's his birthday. So some of the others have arrived already, eh? Who's up there?'

'His employer, sir, a Mrs. Van Huizen. A charming lady, and very wealthy, too.

Then his brother called.'

'Oh, really? Alec's arrived then. That's splendid.'

It sounded as though half the population of Monkton City was holding a meeting in Hillier's room right at that moment.

'The number is seven-o-five, sir.' The clerk leaned across the desk. 'Such a regular patron, Mr. Hillier. Perhaps he would not be offended if we sent up champagne? With the compliments of the management, of course.'

'Well, I believe Mr. Hillier would appreciate that very much.' I checked my watch. 'It's a little early yet. Shall we say around eleven?'

'Eleven it shall be, sir. I shall attend to it personally.'

He watched me with delighted approval as I strode across to the elevators, en route to wish Mr. Hillier many happy returns of the day. I disembarked at seventh and the boy pointed out the door I wanted. I thanked him, walked down the corridor and tapped. There was no reply. I tried the handle and the door opened inwards. At least it started that way then jammed. I pushed, but couldn't open it any further. There was just room for me to squeeze in. Nobody took a shot at me as I closed the door. Dean Willman Hillier was sitting in a deep chair facing the door. On a small table by his outstretched hand was a coffee cup, but the stuff saturating the front of his cream-coloured shirt was not coffee. Three black holes formed a rough triangle on his chest, and the thick, dark blood oozed slowly from the three angles. Whatever Hillier might have told me, I was going to have to find out some other way. At my feet was the reason the door hadn't opened wide. Denver Morley was stretched out on the carpet, the back of his head matted with blood. I checked the rest of the place. Nobody was standing inside any cupboards waiting to blow holes in me. There was no sign of Marcia Van Huizen. Then I went back to Morley and knelt beside him. His heartbeat was steady and although there was a nasty split in his skull, I decided he'd live. Inside his jacket I felt the hard outline of a gun. I pulled out an Italian .32 and sniffed at the muzzle. Hillier hadn't come by his holes from that direction, at least. I was about to put the heater back where it came from, when I had second thoughts and slipped it in the waistband of my pants. Hillier rated a private bathroom. I soaked a towel in some water and started dabbing at the back of Morley's head. After a while he groaned and rolled on to his side.

'C'mon, snap it up, Morley.'

He opened one eye and stared up at me. Then he winced and brought a hand up to poke at the back of his head. I handed him the bloodstained towel. Slowly he sat up.

'All right, let's have it,' I said impatiently.

Then he caught sight of Hillier across the room. If he was pale before, he looked like a death's head now.

'Is that him? That Hillier?' he asked.

I didn't feel we were getting on any too fast.

'Look, Morley. This is Hillier's room. I just came in. I found him like that and

273

you taking a rest on the floor. When I go to a party, I don't like people asking me to point out the host. Now get on with the tale. What're you doing here?'

'I was slugged. Just got inside — '

'I don't mean what are you doing on the floor. I can work that bit out. How did you come to be here at all?'

The damp towel had stopped the flow of blood from the cut on his head.

'Came to see Hillier. It was him brought Cheryl to this lousy town.'

'How do you know that?'

He felt in his pockets for a cigarette, found out the .32 was missing. I pulled it half-way from my pocket and let him see it. He shrugged, pulled out a crumpled pack of Luckys and gave me one.

'I picked up her stuff from the police. I'm the next of kin, you know,' he said bitterly. 'Among it there was a ticket stub from a railroad station deposit boxes. I went down there, picked up a small case. There wasn't much in it, just personal things. But there was this letter. From Hillier.'

'Go on.'

'It was dated last week. He wrote and said he was sorry about her trouble, but he'd help all he could. He sent her a hundred dollars and told her to get to Monkton as soon as she could and call on him here.'

I dragged on the cigarette.

'Why would he do that? Did he know her?'

'How do I know? I told you she was kind of secretive about her friends.'

'O.K., leave that for now. You read the letter, then what?'

'I got over here to the hotel. I didn't want to frighten Hillier away, so I told the guy downstairs I was his brother. I gave him five bucks.'

So I'd been wrong about the clerk. I wouldn't have figured him for a five-man.

'I came straight up here, knocked on the door. A woman called for me to come in. I opened the door, stepped inside, and blooey. That's all I know. How come you showed up anyhow?'

'Kind of wanted a few friendly words with brother Hillier myself. He won't be telling us much now,' I jerked my thumb towards the corpse in the chair.

Morley nodded glumly.

'What about the dame? The one who spoke to me. I guess she did this, huh?'

'I guess so. What time did you show her the back of your head?'

He thought it over, still sitting on the carpet with his legs crossed in front of him.

'Say ten minutes from the railroad station, maybe another five dickering with the fancy pants downstairs. Nine o'clock, five after, no more.'

So I'd missed all the excitement by ten minutes.

'You O.K. now? Fit to get out of here?'

'I think so.' He pulled himself to his feet, wincing each time a movement jarred his head. 'What about him?'

'What about him?' I replied. 'He's not going anywhere.'

'I don't like it much. Don't seem right walking out on a dead man. We ought to call the police.'

'I'll call 'em,' I told him, 'but we don't want to stay here and get mixed up in this. It'll waste too much time. There's

276

something I want you to do. We're going for a ride. I'll tell you on the way.'

'I don't know,' he protested. 'Where we going?'

'To pick up your sister's killer.'

After that I got no more arguments from Morley. As we left the hotel, the counter clerk was busy at a sorting rack, back turned to the door. We climbed into the car and drove away. I told Morley to keep his eyes skinned for a pay-phone, but spotted one myself first. I got through to the local precinct and told them what they'd find in Room 705 at the Hotel Apache. The desk sergeant sounded surprised when I told him my name and address. Most of his information was phoned in by a guy named well-wisher. He wanted to argue when I said I was on my way somewhere else, but pretty soon he found himself holding a dead phone. I had to get some more small change from Morley for the next call, the one to the Van Huizen home. A man said huskily,

'Yeah?'

'Lieutenant Rourke there? The name is Preston.'

'Hang on, I'll see.'

There was a noise like a man walking away from a telephone, then silence, then more noise like a man walking towards a telephone.

'Preston? What's up?'

'Plenty. Listen hard, John.'

I started talking. I told him about what had happened at the Hotel Apache. He didn't interrupt once till I'd finished.

'And you figure she's on her way here right now?' he queried.

'That's what I figure. I've been wrong, but not this time.'

'O.K. I'll be waiting for her. Harrigan, too. By the way, Harrigan said for me to tell you about a certain autopsy.'

'Go ahead and tell me.'

'He got a report a few minutes back. There was a drug, I can't pronounce it, but it has a damn great big name. This is for insomniacs. Seems the late Van Huizen had swallowed enough to put the average wild bull in a coma.'

'I see,' I muttered. 'Then some friendly soul shoved the gun up into his mouth, and we know the rest.'

'Check. Say, how about this other guy, this Morley?' asked Rourke.

'Right here with me, John. We'll be at the house as fast as the traffic laws allow us.'

Back in the car Morley was silent for a time and I was able to concentrate on avoiding the through-town traffic. When we finally hit the outskirts, he turned to me.

'What's all this to you, Preston?'

'I'm getting paid. Van Huizen hired something done. Before I even got started, the man was dead. I've been played for a sucker plenty of times, but somehow I never quite get used to it.'

'Guess I had this cock-eyed. This Van Huizen now, it wasn't him and Cheryl, huh?'

A yellow Buick shot out of an intersection. I yanked on the wheel and closed my eyes. When I opened them, the Buick was fifty yards behind, its front bumper playing post-office with the radiator of a large oil truck. I said something that would have done nothing for the driver's ego, then remembered the question.

'No, my guess is that Van Huizen never heard of Cheryl. The guy responsible for your sister being the way she was is an ex-fighter. Name of Eddie Newman.'

'Newman? That's the guy you shot last night, isn't it? I heard something on the radio.'

'This morning,' I said tersely. 'And he made me shoot. The guy was going to kill me.'

Morley looked at me curiously.

'What're you making excuses for? You know it's O.K. with me if you ripped him up with a meat hook. Is he gonna live?'

His tone wasn't exactly hopeful.

'I don't know yet. We have to get something straight. Ed Newman didn't kill Cheryl, and unless I'm a mile off the beam, he didn't know a thing about her death until he read it in the paper.'

'But you said he was the kid's father?'

'Yeah, I said that. He was. I'm not saying that's anything to brag about, but it isn't murder.'

He didn't seem too convinced about that, and I didn't blame him. The law is the law. A guy who gets a girl a certain way is not the same kind of offender as a guy who kills somebody. But the law isn't the girl's brother. Denver Morley was.

'If he pulls through, I'll kill him myself.'

He said it in a matter-of-fact tone, the same tone he'd used when he came to the Parkside Towers. If he'd raved and shouted, I could have calmed him down. But Morley was cold angry, and that's the worst kind there is. After that he didn't offer any more conversation until we hit the signboard pointing to the Van Huizen place.

'Say, this Van Huizen really had it big, huh?'

'Some.'

I turned up the long drive, remembered in time the sharp right-angle turn at the far end, and slowed down to allow for it.

'That's a crazy idea,' muttered my companion. 'Man with his pedal through the floor would go straight through that hedge.'

I made no answer as I rolled into the open before the house. A little whistle from my right told me that the Van

Huizen residence was having the effect that had been included in the purchase price. There were five cars parked, including Rourke's and a grey farm wagon marked in large letters 'County Sheriff — Official.' We slammed the doors.

'Don't say a lot in there,' I warned. 'Keep listening to me. When I go into my spiel, back me up, will you?'

'You call it, brother. Whatever you say, after what you've done for me.'

The front door was ajar. Inside a plain-clothes man sat in a chair reading the sports pages. I'd seen him around. He looked us over without interest, then jerked his head towards the library.

'Everybody's in there,' he announced.

'Do something for me, will you? Get Rourke out here,' I asked him.

He looked aggrieved.

'I'm a butler now? Oh, O.K., O.K.'

Reluctantly he dragged himself up from the chair. The back of his jacket had got pushed up while he was sitting, and was now hooked over the grip of the police special sticking out of his hip pocket. He poked his head around the library door, and said something. Rourke came out at once.

'Hello, Mark. This Morley?'

I introduced them and they shook briefly. Then Rourke got back to me.

'You sure about this?'

'I'm sure. Marcia's in there?'

'Yep. Like we agreed. Harrigan don't go for this, but he's willing to listen, on account of it's you doing the talking.'

'I'll keep it interesting. Let's go in.'

The Lieutenant led the way inside, then Morley. I brought up the rear. Harrigan sat behind the big desk with the leather top. We nodded, and I thought only a hardened cop would have sat in that particular chair. Marcia Van Huizen was hunched up in a small cane chair by the wall. She looked like hell, and her hands were twitching at the scrap of white handkerchief that lay on her lap. The other side of the desk from Harrigan sat Rona Parsons. She was pleased to see me, and the red lips parted over the gleaming teeth when I walked in. In some ways it compensated for the contempt on Marcia's face. The front of her dress was so low, I half expected to see her feet.

'Well, hallo, Rona. I didn't expect to see you here,' I greeted her.

'Hallo yourself. I called in to see Dean Hillier.'

'I didn't know you knew Hillier?' I made it a question.

'You're forgetting he was Ben's private secretary. He knew all about me.' She said it with no false modesty. The same level tone that I'd liked before.

'I was forgetting that. Say, where is Hillier anyhow?'

'You know quite well where he is. I told you late last night. He's staying at the Hotel Apache,' snapped Marcia.

'So you did, Marcia. It just isn't my day for remembering things. Come to think of it, I saw Hillier this morning. Needed to have a talk with him about one or two little things. Trouble was somebody had a talk with him first. They did their talking with a gun.'

'You — you mean, he's dead? Dean is dead?' Marcia almost screamed.

'Don't sound so surprised, Marcia.' I turned, facing her. 'The man at the desk told me Mrs. Van Huizen was with him when I arrived at the hotel.'

'Man at the desk?' she whispered.

'Yup. He told me Mrs. Van Huizen was up in Hillier's room. Also a man, representing himself as Hillier's brother. In fact, his name is Morley, and he's the brother of Cheryl Vickers, who was the first to die in this business. This is Morley, right here.' I indicated him with a hand.

Morley bowed slightly to no one in particular. He was all keyed up, eyes roving from one to another in the room.

'When I went up to Hillier's room, I found him dead, shot. Morley was on the floor, but he'd only had a clunk on the head. Got it as he stepped inside the door. A woman hit him from behind. But he saw her face. There's a mirror on the wall opposite the door. Morley saw the woman just as she hit him. And do you know something? It wasn't Marcia Van Huizen at all. It was you, Rona.'

Everybody looked at Rona Parsons.

She went white, then laughed shortly.

'You're crazy, Preston. You're making the whole thing up, you and this man.'

'No, lady,' said Morley quietly. 'No mistake. I saw you in the mirror.'

'It's a lie,' she spat. 'There is no mirror on — '

Then she stopped. The room was very still. Rona dived into her purse and came out with the little .22 I remembered. It was all over very fast. Morley flung himself the seven feet between them. The midget gun cracked once, then the two of them were on the floor, the .22 knocked violently from Rona's hand. It slithered across the desk and Harrigan's large fist closed over it. I jumped to pull Morley off Rona before he killed her, but there was no fight in him at all. The tiny slug had gone into his stomach and his blood was welling all over the tan suit Rona Parsons was wearing. As I gently pulled him off her, she lay there staring in horror at the sticky mess on her jacket.

'This guy needs a doctor, very fast,' I snapped.

Marcia suddenly came to life.

'I'll call Doctor Parkins. He's only a few minutes from here.'

She went to the telephone. Morley was trying to say something. His lips were working, but I couldn't make any sense out of it.

'Don't try to move him,' ordered Rourke, 'he's best where he is till the doc gets here.'

Harrigan didn't say anything at all. He was watching Rona Parsons, who still lay stiff on the floor, staring unbelievingly at Morley's blood. Harrigan said suddenly,

'Why should a little blood upset you? You've been spilling plenty of it.'

She said nothing. Harrigan exclaimed in disgust and went over to the door.

'Gus, c'm in here. Pick up the shrinking violet there and take her down to the station. Attempted murder.' He turned to Rourke. 'That O.K. with you, Rourke? I mean let's get her behind bars on something. We can argue about the big charges later.'

'Sure, that's O.K.,' replied John.

Gus bent down and grabbed Rona Parsons by the arm. She made no protest as he helped her to her feet. It was as though she'd been struck dumb. She looked at me as she was led out, but there was no recognition in her eyes.

'What do you make of it, Harrigan?' queried Rourke.

'I dunno. A queer finish. Looks to me as if she's building up for a temporary insanity plea already.'

'Could be,' John agreed. 'Anyway, did you get that shape? I've got ten bucks says we'll never get a maximum penalty against a dame who looks like that.'

'No bet. I've been in this racket too long,' was the reply.

Morley was trying to talk again. I bent right over, putting my ear to his lips.

' — get her?' he managed.

'Sure, sure we got her. Thanks to you. You ought to get a medal,' I told him.

He worked his face around into what could have been a grin. Rourke and Harrigan were whispering together. I couldn't hear the words, but it didn't take a mindreader to know they were assessing Morley's chances, and not liking the odds. We all stayed that way, until Parkins arrived, a gaunt, sad-faced man who didn't waste any time on words. He cut away the clothing around Morley's wound. After a while he stood up and looked at us.

'This man can't be moved. He's lost too much blood already. I can't risk his being bounced around in an ambulance.'

'Can't you do anything for him, Doc?' asked Harrigan.

Parkins looked over at him coldly.

'Certainly I can. I've got to get that piece of metal out of him. Now. My nurse is in the car outside. Send her in here, please. Everybody else outside. I must have absolute quiet.'

I had a feeling this Parkins knew what he was doing. He gave me confidence, somehow. We all filed out, Rourke going to the front door to call the nurse in. Marcia showed us into the room where we'd all spent so many hours on the night her husband died. There seems to be a rule about these things. Marcia and I both sat in the same chairs we'd occupied last time. Harrigan and Rourke found places to park.

'How'd you figure this, Preston? We both got warrants with another name on 'em.' This was from Harrigan.

I looked at Marcia. Now that the excitement was over, she'd gone back to the lost-looking girl I'd seen when I arrived.

'I only knew one thing for sure,' I answered, 'and that was that I'd been set up as a patsy in this from the start. A man came and hired me in a blackmail case. The same night the blackmailer is murdered and the victim commits suicide. That I didn't go for. I was a star attraction. Sure the man was being blackmailed, you can ask Mark Preston, the private dick. He was hired to get the girl to lay off. It stank.'

'There was that note you showed me,' Wilson pointed out. 'That was certainly written by Benedict Van Huizen.'

'I have an idea about that note, too,' I pulled it out of my pocket and passed it over. 'You notice there's no date on it. That's Point One. Point Two is that my name doesn't appear.'

'It says here 'the man P.'' objected Wilson.

'Agreed. Lots of guys have names beginning with the letter P. George Porter for one.'

Rourke tapped the note with his forefinger, thoughtfully.

'You think this could refer to Porter?'

'Could be. I think Porter suddenly got back into the money and where he got it was from Dean Hillier. Hillier was authorised to draw on his boss's private account.'

'But what for? I mean, why should Hillier hire a guy like Porter for anything?'

I tapped an Old Favourite from the pack and stuck it in my face.

'George Porter was an ex-cop. You remember Schultz thought he knew Hillier from somewhere? I naturally assumed it would have to be from some newspaper shot or other. Then I got to thinking. It seemed there could be a connection between Porter and Hillier. Schultz thought he knew Hillier's face. I began to wonder whether Porter had ever put the arm on Hillier for anything. If he had, there'd be a picture somewhere on the department files. Schultz only just finished his rookie assignment including one month of doing nothing but looking at mug-shots all day and every day.'

'It begins to figure,' breathed Rourke. 'And you found such a picture?'

I nodded.

'I went down to the crime vault in the Globe Offices. Porter arrested a man named Hillier in an attempted extortion case three years ago. It was one of those deals where the dame gets herself tangled up with a married man in good standing at the bank. When she has the sucker all steamed up, along comes the hero, Hillier this time. He's her husband and if the chump doesn't want his name all over the front page, et cetera. So the chump antes up. Only this one didn't. He hollered copper. The copper was Porter, the phoney husband was Hillier.'

'And the wife was Rona Parsons?' suggested Harrigan.

'Seems likely now. She skipped out the first time. There was no photograph of her, nothing but a name, Ivy Hart.'

'What happened to Hillier?' asked Rourke in an interested tone.

'Nothing. After putting the department to a lot of expense and trouble, the turkey refused to prosecute. Said it would all come out and he'd be ruined just the same.'

'It happens every day,' interjected Harrigan.

'Yeah. So Hillier walked out a free man, and presumably went to find Ivy Hart. I imagine the pair of them would have given Monkton City the cold shoulder for the next few years. Then they got a chance at Benedict Van Huizen, and with that kind of money at stake, they evidently thought the old town was cool enough for a return trip. Ivy, or Rona as we know her, went to work on Van Huizen. She had the looks and the class to do it. Maybe at first they intended to do their usual act, but then they must have decided this was the big one. Maybe she could even get to marry the guy. Anyway, they got greedy. Hillier, remember, was no ordinary cheap chiseller. He had a good appearance and a college education, just the kind of man to be private secretary to somebody in Van Huizen's position.'

'I get the drift,' put in Rourke. 'Hillier lands the job with Van Huizen. Just when he's all set, George Porter recognises him and holds on for free meals.'

'That's how I see it. Naturally Hillier didn't have any money himself. Not the kind of money to keep a guy like Porter quiet. So he pitched his employer some tale about a job that needed doing, any job, and got Porter on the payroll that way.'

'And managed to work it so that Van Huizen had to write him a note to do it,' said Harrigan, who had been listening with both ears.

I shrugged and the straight line of blue smoke from my cigarette jerked like an Eastern dancer.

'I don't know, but somehow I don't think so. The note was just a break. A guy with a twisted mind like Hillier would be able to see future possibilities in a note like that. All he needed when the time came was a fall guy whose name started with a P. I drew the short match.'

Rourke stood up, yawned, and stretched his arms over his head.

'I could sleep for a month,' he announced. 'But this looks like being a busy day. There's a big hole in all this, Preston. Why should Hillier and the girl kill the goose that laid the golden egg? Don't make any sense.'

'I don't think the girl was in that. Hillier had a big fault for a con man. He gambled. He was in to Kalmus for fourteen thousand until last week-end.'

'And he suddenly paid up by drawing on his boss's private account,' put in Rourke.

'On Friday. He knew Van Huizen would get a query from the bank, but that wouldn't happen till Monday, Tuesday if he was lucky, so he had two clear days to work out what he was going to do. He'd been expecting to have to do something of the kind anyhow, because he'd already sent for Cheryl Morley.'

Harrigan crossed one leg over the other

and passed a finger along the crease in his pants.

'Maybe it's lack of sleep with me, but I don't get the bit about the girl. How could they hope to get away with this stuff about 'you are the father of my child'?'

'They didn't,' I told him. 'The whole thing was Hillier's plant. The girl didn't know a thing about it. She thought Hillier was going to help her put some pressure on Ed Newman.'

At the mention of his name, Marcia's knuckles whitened as she gripped the handkerchief. It was the first sign we'd had she was even listening.

'You mean Hillier wrote the blackmail note himself?' This was from Rourke.

'I'm sure of it. It would have come here with the morning mail. Mrs. Van Huizen could tell us about that. I suppose your husband would be in the habit of looking at anything important before leaving for the office?'

I was staring right at her as I spoke. She had no alternative but to look back at me. There was no expression either on her face or in her words.

'Dean would open the mail in the mornings. If there was anything my husband should know about, he would show him after breakfast.'

'And this blackmail note happened like that?'

'Yes. My husband just laughed at first, but Dean pointed out what a lot of unfavourable publicity could result from anything of that kind. It wasn't a convenient time.'

'Exactly. So your husband left it to Hillier to handle, if possible. If not, he'd have to take a hand himself.'

'That was more or less the gist of what was said,' she agreed.

'Thank you. Well, that was the way Mr. Dean Willman Hillier set it up,' I turned back to the two police officers. 'Tuesday morning he triggered the thing off by calling on the patsy named P something. Me.'

Rourke was leaning up against the wall.

'I been thinking. Hillier arrived soon after the shot. I figure it like this. First he killed the girl in town. Then he came up the drive and cut his lights. That stupid hedge, where you have to throw the wheel right over to approach the house, that would hide a car just fine. Then he walked around to the back of the house, let himself in through the window which he'd left open. Benedict Van Huizen wouldn't think there was anything strange in that. After all, Hillier did live here. Van Huizen was in the habit of taking a drink before he went to bed, so Hillier managed to slip the dope in his whisky. When he passed out it was a simple matter to stick the gun in his mouth and it was all over.'

'That sounds all right,' objected Harrigan, 'but why take all that trouble? Why not just kill the guy and have done with it?'

'Because a murder is a murder. The police don't care for it at all,' I reminded him. 'It's my guess he wanted to make it look as if the murderer was faking a suicide. He left a couple of things around, the glass for one, a cigarette butt and scarf belonging to Mrs. Van Huizen. Anybody would have agreed that on the face of it she was a first-class suspect, and on top of that she had no real alibi for the crucial time. Hillier had made sure of that already. He'd fixed for a noisy crowd to play at the Club. He knew Marcia wouldn't want to stick around while they were there. I don't think he meant her any harm. With the kind of money she has at her disposal, some witness would eventually be found who would swear to her whereabouts at the crucial time.'

'So you figure the stuff was planted as delaying action while he beat it?' asked Rourke.

'I do. Trouble was, of course, there was still George Porter. He would have guessed right away that Hillier knew something. As a sideline he'd been taking money from Newman on the understanding he wouldn't tell Mrs. Van Huizen about Cheryl Morley. When Porter heard about the two deaths, he knew one thing for sure. He was on the spot. From where he was sitting it had to be either Hillier or Newman who was responsible. He couldn't go to the police and he'd seen my name mentioned in the paper. He knew he could talk to me and I'd listen without repeating it over the radio, so after hiding up for twenty-four hours, he came to me in the middle of the night. He figured that would be a safe bet. But he had to get greedy. Had to take one last bite at Ed Newman. Hillier must have seen him at the Club.'

Rourke pursed his lips and a short whistle came out.

'Porter too, eh? I got a routine report of a hit and run.'

'Mrs. Van Huizen, did Hillier have the loan of one of the family cars?' I asked.

She thought about it briefly.

'Why, yes. He knew he could always take a car if it wasn't needed.'

'Thank you. One of your cars was parked outside the Club Rendezvous shortly after Porter's accident. There were fresh scratches along the bodywork and the front fender was damaged. The car Mrs. Van Huizen had out there at the same time was a different model. I think Rona Parsons had a hand in that one. Hillier would have told her the story when she came to Monkton yesterday. It had been a big shock to him when the

300

Sheriff's Office called Van Huizen's death a suicide.'

Harrigan coughed and fiddled with his shirt cuffs. I felt sorry for him, but not too much. Knowing Dunphy was such a bad boy, he ought to have checked his work more thoroughly. Every step.

'Last night he even wanted to see me,' I went on. 'I had to postpone his first offer. Second time around he didn't show. It's my guess he was jumpy about the missing leads. Wanted to tell me he'd noticed the scarf or something. His lady friend talked him out of it during the evening.'

'Him and the girl probably figured the Sheriff was playing some deep game,' pointed out Harrigan. 'One thing about being on the right side of the law, you always get the other side thinking you're doing a lot of complicated thinking they can't even guess at.'

'Yes,' I agreed. 'They were sure you'd have picked up the evidence that was lying around and were just waiting your time to grab Mrs. Van Huizen. That was when Rona thought she'd found her way out. She could see Hillier was in a bad way. Once the police got around to him, he wouldn't have lasted ten minutes, and she'd find herself looking at those grey walls, too. So she figured to clinch it for the police by repeating the dose. Hillier murdered by Marcia, who would then commit suicide.'

Marcia looked up sharply.

'You mean that woman came here to — to kill me?' she said hoarsely.

'That's about it. You were about the same size, same colouring. The identification at the hotel would have been fairly safe. You noticed her dress?'

Her lip curled slightly.

'I noticed that she hardly had anything on at all above the waist, if that's what you mean.'

'That's what I mean,' I assured her. 'And that's why she had that dress on. The desk clerk could have been phased on her facial characteristics because he wasn't looking in that direction. But the dress would be enough for him to take on oath. And you would have been wearing that dress when they found you.'

She shuddered. Rourke said.

'Well, I've got a lot to do. So've you, Preston. Everybody wants statements from you.'

Harrigan got to his feet now.

'That is true enough. Where do you want to start?'

It was twenty miles ride whichever way I headed.

'Think I'll take the Sheriff first. I want to watch him squirming anyway.'

'Suit yourself,' he shrugged. 'Got a car here?'

'Yeah. You get started, I'll be along about twenty minutes behind you.'

He went out followed by Rourke, who stood in the open doorway and said:

'Oh, and Mark, don't come downtown before this evening, huh? I'm going to question a bed all the afternoon.'

When the door closed, Marcia spoke.

'Well, I suppose you expect congratulations of some sort, Mr. Preston? And there'll be the matter of your fee, won't there? How much do you usually charge for shooting down an innocent man?'

I bit back what I'd been going to say and waited five seconds.

'After our last talk, I thought we were all through rubbing sparks off each other. Now I'm going to tell you about what happened with Ed Newman. And you, Marcia?' I shouted her down as she began to say something. 'You are going to shut up and listen.'

She subsided. For a moment she looked almost frightened as though I might start shooting again any minute. Okay, let her think it. It was time Mark Preston got a fair hearing around here.

'I went to see Newman this morning. He was edgy, to put it mildly. I asked him a few things and the next I knew, he was holding a large automatic on me. The guy was all tensed up, he would have killed me all right. This I'm allergic to. I made my play and I was lucky. It was Newman who went out on the stretcher.'

'I heard it on the radio. Why you're — '

'Shut up! I'm going to tell you some bits that weren't on the radio,' I snarled. 'Ed Newman was being black-mailed by George Porter. You heard me tell those guys just now. He told you a yarn about information being given to your husband.

He had to tell you something and the truth would not have been well received. Then there are these two murders, Cheryl and your husband. Put yourself in Ed's position. He figured that somehow you had found out about Cheryl and had taken your own way out.'

'But that's ridiculous,' she protested. 'How could he think — '

'Will you please be quiet? While Ed was thinking all this over, he had a visitor. Dunphy, the sergeant who was here with Harrigan that night. He had one of your cigarette butts and a scarf of yours, both found in the library just after the murder. Newman gave him a thousand dollars for them. Now he was sure you were guilty. So when I came prying around, he couldn't take any chances. He thought I was on to you.'

'I see. And you really think he meant to kill you?' She was almost convinced.

'In this business a man develops kind of a feeling for these things. Either that or he goes out of business. In a horizontal position. Ed would have killed me all right.'

She stood up. The handkerchief was still getting some rough treatment from both hands as she walked up and down.

'I'm just a private dick, not a lonely hearts' counsellor, but I'm going to tell you something just the same. I believe Newman loves you. Not the way they write about it maybe, with the string orchestra and the orange blossoms, but a way where he'll fight for you, even if you don't know about it. Was a time when, if anybody asked me what Ed Newman was doing around a girl with several million dollars, I'd have said several million dollars-worth of business. But when I looked down the wrong end of that thirty-eight this morning, I changed my mind. He was going to kill me, just for you.'

'That's the truth, Mr. Preston?'

'That's the truth, lady. It's not every day I spoil my own chance with a rich woman by putting in a plug for somebody else.'

There were tears in her eyes as she stood in front of me. I patted her on the arm.

'When did you last call the hospital?' I asked.

'Just before you arrived. They said he was out of danger, but would be weak for several days yet.'

I bent down and kissed her quickly on the mouth. She was surprised, but didn't draw away.

'Why did you do that?'

'Damned if I know. Relief, I guess. Believe me, Ed didn't give me any alternative this morning. It was him or me, but that didn't make me feel any easier. I feel fine now.'

I meant it. Even the tiredness seemed to have worn off. Now that the strain between us was gone, she wanted to ask a lot of questions. I didn't mind too much, but I had to call a halt in the end. I'd promised Harrigan I'd be right behind him, and there was a reason for me to be sure I was back in Monkton City by two-thirty in the afternoon. At the heavy front door she said,

'Goodbye. We didn't get on very well most of the time, did we?'

'No. I guess it's a matter of chemistry.

Anyhow, we can keep out of each other's way now.'

She held out her hand.

'I think that might be the best thing. When you're around I get this nervous reaction. And I think you do, too.'

I knew what she meant. Her hand was cool and firm. As I rolled behind the high hedge, she was standing at the door, watching.

10

Somewhere a clock chimed three. I climbed out of the car and went in through the glass doors. A man dressed in a black suit with a black tie stood just inside the door. His face was solemn and with a slow movement of his arm, he gestured me through a small door at the side of the room. I went through. The smell of incense was very strong here. A guy who could have been the twin brother of the one outside motioned me to a seat. There was no one else in the chapel but the two of us.

It was quite a short ceremony, but I thought it impressive, and I was glad to be there. When it was over, the hidden organ rose to a crescendo, and the mahogany box rolled smoothly towards the wall. A section of wall rose sound-lessly and the box slid behind into the darkness. Then the panel closed again and the music died away. I rose and made my way out, man number two holding the door for me. In the first room, man number one bowed very slightly.

'I trust everything was to your satisfaction?' His voice was hushed.

'Thank you. Everything was fine.'

He coughed very slightly, but in that place it sounded like a gun going off.

'I beg your pardon, are you perhaps one of the family?'

'Er — no. No. I just thought — well, I just thought. It seemed to me somebody ought to — '

'Quite so. I understand. Let us hope she finds her peace now.'

Outside the sun seemed very strong after the shadowed chapel. I took out a cigarette and lit it, drawing the smoke deep down inside me. Behind was the gloom and in front was the sunlit street. Maybe that's what it's all about, for all I know. I was glad I'd been, anyhow.

I guess you could say I really saw Cheryl Vickers twice.

We do hope that you have enjoyed reading this large print book.

Did you know that all of our titles are available for purchase?

We publish a wide range of high quality large print books including:
Romances, Mysteries, Classics
General Fiction
Non Fiction and Westerns

Special interest titles available in large print are:
The Little Oxford Dictionary
Music Book, Song Book
Hymn Book, Service Book

Also available from us courtesy of Oxford University Press:
Young Readers' Dictionary
(large print edition)
Young Readers' Thesaurus
(large print edition)

For further information or a free brochure, please contact us at:
Ulverscroft Large Print Books Ltd.,
The Green, Bradgate Road, Anstey,
Leicester, LE7 7FU, England.
Tel: (00 44) **0116 236 4325**
Fax: (00 44) **0116 234 0205**

SEA VENGEANCE

Robert Charles

Chief Officer John Steele was disillusioned with his ship; the *Shantung* was the slowest old tramp on the China Seas, and her Captain was another fading relic. The *Shantung* sailed from Saigon, the port of war-torn Vietnam, and was promptly hijacked by the Viet Cong. John Steele, helped by the lovely but unpredictable Evelyn Ryan, gave them a much tougher fight than they had expected, but it was Captain Butcher who exacted a final, terrible vengeance.

HIRE ME A HEARSE

Piers Marlowe

Whenever Wilma Haven decided to be wayward, she insisted that she was seen to be wayward. So perhaps she was merely being consistent when she hired a hearse before committing suicide, then proceeded to take her time over the act in a very public place. However, Wilma died not from her own act, but by the murderous intent of an unsuspected killer, and Superintendent Frank Drury of Scotland Yard becomes embroiled in his most challenging case ever.